OWL CANYON
PRESS

7177 Overbrook Drive • Niwot, Colorado 80503

D1367055

Emily Greenhouse
The New York Review of Books
435 Hudson Street, Suite 300
New York, NY 10014
RE: *The Suffering of Lesser Mammals* by Greg Sanders Owl Canyon Press (April 15, 2022)

March 8, 2022

Dear Ms. Greenhouse:

I am pleased to enclose a copy of our forthcoming title, *The Suffering of Lesser Mammals* by Greg Sanders. Greg is the author of the story collection *Motel Girl* and numerous works of fiction and non-fiction. He and his family live in New York, where he earns his living as a technical writer. In a review of *Motel Girl* for American Book Review (May/June 2009) Scott Elliott wrote, "The stories aspire to the have-your-cake-and-eat-it-too achievement of

FOR IMMEDIATE RELEASE

Owl Canyon Press Announces

Coming April 15, 2022

The Suffering of Lesser Mammals
by Greg Sanders

PRAISE FOR *The Suffering of Lesser Mammals*

"Greg Sanders is a startling fiction writer with a quirky-snarky & deeply affecting prose manner that's original and all his own. I highly recommend you jump on his new collection of stories, *The Suffering of Lesser Mammals*. Of which we are some."

—**Frederick Barthelme**, author of the story collection *Moon Deluxe*, the novel *There Must Be Some Mistake*, and fourteen other books in between.

"Greg Sanders is a beguiling, far-ranging fabulist, whose wily, hyper-smart inventions take us from Big Sur to Brooklyn, from Kafka's Prague to a remote exoplanet—and to cyberspace, whose cold zones measure human value in 'clickthrough rates,' and whose dark corners register 'a world in magnificent turmoil and unrepentant decline.'"

David Gates, Pulitzer finalist and author of *A Hand Reached Down to Guide Me*

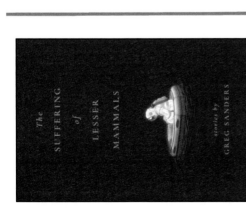

The Suffering of Lesser Mammals
by Greg Sanders

April 15 2022

978-1-952085-11-6

152 | 6x9 | $18.95
Trade Paperback

For more information:
Publisher: Gene Hayworth
720.412.1548
gene@owlcanyonpress.com

In *The Suffering of Lesser Mammals*, acclaimed author Greg Sanders draws the reader into a world of believable absurdity, as individual crises meld with those of the age. Among the thirteen stories in this collection, a young father's anxiety throws the Earth out of orbit; a bachelor breaks up with his car; a "multivariate correlator" conjures a lonely deity; two sisters are abducted by a cadre of immortal alewives. Wildly inventive, morally wise, and achingly funny, this is the short story as reimagined by a fearless—and fearsome—voice.

ABOUT THE AUTHOR

Greg Sanders is the author of the story collection *Motel Girl* and numerous works of fiction and non-fiction. He and his family live in New York, where he earns his living as a technical writer.

Owl Canyon Press
7177 Overbrook Drive
Niwot, CO 80503

Distributed by:

Baker & Taylor
1120 US Highway 22 E.
Bridgewater, NJ 08807
800 775-1800

YBP Library Services
999 Maple St.
Contoocook, NH 03229
800-258-3774

Ingram Book Company
(615) 213-7015
www.ingrambook.com

Brodart Company
500 Arch Street
Williamsport, Pa. 17701
570-326-2461

www.owlcanyonpress.com

existing in both literal and symbolic realms. Many of them reach this rare ground.

In *The Suffering of Lesser Mammals* Sanders draws the reader into a world of believable absurdity, as individual crises meld with those of the age. Among the thirteen stories in this collection, a young father's anxiety throws the Earth out of orbit; a bachelor breaks up with his car; a "multivariate correlator" conjures a lonely deity; two sisters are abducted by a cadre of immortal alewives. Wildly inventive, morally wise, and achingly funny, this is the short story as reimagined by a fearless—and fearsome—voice.

I hope that you will consider assigning *The Suffering of Lesser Mammals* for review in *The New York Review of Books*.

Sincerely,

Gene Hayworth
Owl Canyon Press
gene@owlcanyonpress.com

The Suffering of Lesser Mammals

Also by Greg Sanders

Motel Girl: Stories

The Suffering of Lesser Mammals

stories by
Greg Sanders

Owl Canyon Press

First Edition, 2022
All Rights Reserved
Library of Congress Cataloging-in-Publication Data

Sanders, Greg
The Suffering of Lesser Mammals —1st ed.
p. cm.

ISBN: 978-1-952085-11-6
Library of Congress Control Number: 2021952716

Owl Canyon Press
Boulder, Colorado

Disclaimer

Acknowledgments

The author extends his thanks to the following publications, in which some of the stories in this collection first appeared (often in different form): "A Blintz on Ross 128b" and "Port Authority" in *New World Writing*; "The Suffering of Lesser Mammals" in *The Warwick Review*; "Prague's Children" in *H.O.W. Journal*; "A History of Cars" in *Essays & Fictions*.

The author also thanks Galley Begger Press (UK) for publishing "Beta" and "The Fate of Mathematicians" as ebooks, and Social Disease (UK) for including "Neutral" in the anthology *3:AM London, New York, Paris*.

For Margot. Let's make more latkes.

CONTENTS

A History of Cars.. 13

Port Authority.. 21

Beta.. 34

The Fate of Mathematicians 51

Prague's Children... 64

Neutral 76

The Suffering of Lesser Mammals............................ 84

A Blintz on Ross 128b... 100

The Coastal Shelf 111

Bring on the Happies 118

The Visual Display of Qualitative Information 130

Zurich Wins Again... 133

Zymurgium 138

A History of Cars

His head was propped up on two or three pillows, affording him a view of his son reading by the opened bedroom window. Now in his mid-forties, his progeny was lanky and thin, nearly bent double, his face planted in some old novel he'd picked out from the library downstairs. A light September breeze was coming into the room through that window, a breeze scented with the old pines that had protected the house for 150 years. An atheist to the core, the dying man was readying himself for the nothingness he knew awaited him.

He was best known as the creator of *An Illustrated History of Cars*, which captured the imagination of the world when it was published in 1978. The book's original cover depicts a fourteenth century automobile in striking cross-sectional detail. It is one of those iconic illustrations that enters a culture's pictorial vocabulary, like the sailboat and monster on the cover of *Where the Wild Things Are*, or the flame-red horse on *The Catcher in the Rye*. Like all the book's images, the vehicular rendering is the author's handiwork. A trained commercial artist, he performed his visual duties with such unflinching seriousness that many readers of the time came to believe that the first fully functional automobile chugged along during the rule of King James I, and that workable prototypes had been built as early as the reign of Canute the Great. As evidence of this earliest of working vehicles, the book includes a color plate of an eleventh century tapestry showing the horses and carriages of a royal procession. Tucked in among them, a self-propelled four-wheeled cart can be seen releasing a plume of exhaust into the air.

For decades the author had lived by himself in the house in which he was now preparing to fade away—the family's rundown Victorian mansion on a hill overlooking the city of Yonkers. This was a dilapidated castle from which, on pleasant weather weekends, he would flee for his bungalow in the western Catskills. Kids used to sneak into the dense band of woods—littered with bottles, plastic bags, used needles, and the occasional corpse—that surrounded the mansion, waiting for him to make his weekly exodus, wanting to catch a glimpse of the mysterious man. And suddenly there he'd be, emerging into the shadows of the veranda, collapsible cane in hand, a canvas mountaineering backpack from another era hanging from his shoulders. He'd look around as if he knew he were being watched, then duck under the perpetually broken gutter spout to make his escape. He was a tall man, and he bent to get into his old Datsun as if it were a space capsule. It was never known to exactly what destination he was heading, only that it was somewhere "upstate."

He was a widower, and thought often about Jennifer, a celebrated art historian with a lacerating wit, and long legs. They had wed a decade before the book's publication. This was a time of heavy rumination for him, a period during which he had begun to assemble his ideas and make sketches for the book, hunched over a drafting table in the mansion's basement, secretive and over-tired. During this period Jennifer would berate him, claiming he was stuck in another realm and unwilling to "climb out of that dark cave." Indeed, his wife had been onto him, for on those late nights he felt as if he were traveling to another world, that he could see these strange vehicles, the engineers clad in their medieval garb, half-naked smiths working iron and steel and copper with hammers on anvils lighted by great furnaces, all to fashion the components of engines, of axles and springs, steering boxes and ur-transmissions of copper gears and hardwood spindles. Jennifer held on for the ride, adapted to his weirdness, he to her need for absolutism and unambiguous, staccato statements of intent, her censure of adverbs. In 1969 Jennifer bore them a son, Marvin (he by the opened window). And that son, upon his own marriage, fled with his wife to New Zealand. He was back now to help guide his dear old dad up this final exit ramp.

At the apogee of the author's fame, when his book was on the *New York Times* bestseller list and he was on a world book tour, Jennifer was diagnosed with metastatic melanoma, and within a year she was gone. He had met many other women after her death, but was always reminded—always—of what he no longer had, not of what he might gain.

What an obvious and cruel joke, that the boy he loved so much had unambiguously fled from him the moment he'd managed the means to do so, that the kid wanted to get as far away as he could not only from his father, but from the cobwebs of his childhood home and the memories its walls enclosed. Sari, Marvin's wife, also seemed thrilled to have left her clan behind (she hailed from Maine). She and Marvin had convinced themselves that their bond was the shared plight of the wronged and pursued. The author believed this was a fiction, for he and Jennifer had doted to no end on Marvin, their only child, a kid whose sullenness would have tested the best parents of the day. He had sometimes imagined his son and Sari as minuscule figures moving along upside-down on the other side of the planet, doing their domestic chores as he puttered about the big Yonkers house in the middle of the night, alone.

A familiar sentimental haze had enshrouded the author on evenings like that, as he sat in his large library. Before him, filling one wall of shelves, were the predecessors and variations of *An Illustrated History of Cars*: bundles of sketches, uncorrected proofs and advance copies, first editions, all the reprints and translations, and finally the re-issues, which came out in the mid-1990s. This book, it seemed, would be his life's sole artistic accomplishment. Creating it had come of deep inspiration and fixation; it was born of a creative love that most people never get to experience, and he'd known for years that he'd never again feel such fury.

His melancholy had been like an old gray-muzzled dog that followed him around the house and settled at his feet wherever he sat. First, his comparatively bright morning moods would take hold, sparked by sunlight coming in between trees where it could, pushing in through the dusty parlor windows. This would give way to a solemn lunchtime feeling during which he listened to classical music on the radio and ate a simple meal he'd make for himself—a sandwich, or pasta with sauce from a jar. By evening, a downright oppressive mood got its talons into him, a mood in which he could find comfort in nothing of the world but two tall glasses of Scotch. Yet he would not let himself become a full-blown miserable, nor would he allow himself the smallest slip into slovenliness. He drew himself a bath every other night, placed the second glass of whisky on a side table, then lowered himself into the steaming water with a groan that the mice in the walls could hear. This, at least, was pleasurable, to warm the old bones, to be honest with himself about his pale body, the knobby, bluish knees; his silver body hair waving like silk threads underwater. Honesty had always been important to him—an unflinching assessment of self and environment. But what good was this assessment in a vacuum? What good was it if you were still heading inevitably toward vanquishment and dissolution? Thus, drink was always welcome.

His weekend travels helped stanch the melancholic flow for a day or two. The process and labor of getting to the Catskills bungalow distracted him. The drive along the New York State Thruway, then to Route 17 and on toward the elbow of New York State, provided him the opportunity to observe the other cars on the road, the habits of contemporary drivers (they had stopped using indicators around 1984). When he arrived in the spring or summer, the long grass, crushed under the car's tires, would scent the air; birds would flit away from the trees and the nests they'd built under the eaves the moment he unlatched the car door. The memories were sweet—of himself and Jennifer lolling away weekends in the garden, or swimming in the Delaware River, then of their son and his penchant for overturning every stone on their land in search of critters to identify. At the peak of their lives there, before Jennifer was stricken, they were a half-crazed trio filling the place with their frenetic yearnings. The house, nestled between a road and a high ridge, had a stream flowing through its backyard. He had always sympathized with his son's impulse. The decrepit bungalow and the land on which it sat seemed somehow to mirror his own mind, to be full of unexplored niches needing illumination. The labyrinth of tiny cellars beneath their feet, left over from a different era, mirrored the dark spaces of the author's imagination.

During his last trip to the house, the author was confronted with just how diminished he had become. Hours after he arrived on that April afternoon, a powerful thunderstorm rumbled in and broke the calm of the little valley. The electricity in the bungalow went out because of a lightning surge. As the storm went on and on, and the house shook beneath a quivering night sky, he struggled to locate a flashlight, finally finding it in the cupboard under the kitchen sink. Its batteries nearly dead, the light it threw was yellow and shadowy. It took another half hour for him to find a replacement fuse at the back of the odds-and-ends drawer in the little alcove. He then had to find the key to the padlock on the Bilco doors that led to the cellar, upon the far wall of which, as he recalled, the fuse box was mounted.

The rain came down in sheets, the dying flashlight illuminating his arthritic fingers as he tried the odd assortment of keys on the door's padlock. After the third or fourth key, he was able to release the lock and, with some difficulty, lift the door. The flashlight was now dead and he felt his way down the dank steps, visual guidance given by the occasional flash of lightning. Once he set foot on the slab he moved forward in a straight line, aiming for the far wall. Memories and artifacts lurked down here in the darkness. He knew that his son's vintage Flexible Flyer hung on the wall to his right, its runners furry with rust; that the steel rim of an unearthed wagon wheel leaned against another wall; that his wife's ancient gardening implements—a faded straw hat, nested stacks of clay pots, bags of unopened manure—occupied a work table by the boiler. And he knew that other, less definable mementos of his past, bound together by an abstract contract, lay in the distant corners, in the crawl spaces and root cellars that branched off of this main room.

He felt for the fuse box on the far wall and, on touching a surface-mounted steel cabinet, remembered that the electrical service had been upgraded nearly a decade ago, and the fuse box he sought had been replaced by a circuit breaker. The fuse in his pocket was but more evidence of his forgetfulness. He opened the little metal door, clicked the main breaker switch and immediately saw a flash before his eyes. He felt his lower back give way, heard his own yelp of pain, and fell to the floor.

He lay face-up, all but paralyzed. The cellar always flooded during torrential downpours, and soon a shallow plane of cold water gathered around his body. Electricity had not felled him, though it took a few moments for him to realize this. Instead, it was a herniated disc, an ancient affliction making a reprise. Attempt after demoralizing attempt to rise even to his elbows failed. Each time he tried, a shock went through his body and he saw flashes of blue beneath his eyelids.

The water would rise almost to his ears, and then the emergency sump pump in the far corner would click on and push it out of the cellar, clicking off when its float dropped, happily humming into action when it rose again. If he hadn't flicked the circuit breaker on, he realized in a daze, he could have drowned there in his own cellar, among the artifacts of his past. On and on it went through the night, this tidal rise and fall.

Late the next morning a neighbor, seeing the Bilco door ajar from a curve up the road, came to find him ashen and soaked, nearly dead with hypothermia.

It was as if his body awaited this final insult to begin its cascade of failing systems. Before long, all his frailties came to the fore—his enlarged heart, his fossilized arteries, his hypoglycemia, infections of the blood. He rejected a prolonged hospital stay, a "drug-induced idiocy," as he called it. When his prognosis was dim, as dim as could be, his son and daughter-in-law flew in from New Zealand and took up residence in the Yonkers mansion, hovering around the old man during his presumed final weeks. At least he could manage in the bathroom on his own, but he'd been forced to give up drinking, and now he let his son and Sari (who, he realized, resembled the boy's mother) draw his bath, guide him to the tub's edge, then leave him to his own devices.

He wanted to be fearless, for like many, death—his own—had preoccupied him since he became aware of its inevitability more than seven decades ago. The questions were as old as civilization, as painful to ask as a pinprick. How well would he manage to do it in the end? Would he not fall into a panic? He had always imagined some variety of wretched pain along with a loss of perception, then of self, an end that was embarrassing in the complete—indeed ultimate—loss of control. He'd spent the last days lying in bed, fevered, unable to fill his lungs, his heart racing, his mouth dry, his vision playing tricks on him. But he was in many ways more present than he'd ever been, and not in a great deal of pain. Sometimes he'd see that Marvin was in the room, reading by the open window, or looking down at him, holding his hand bedside. Sari was also in and out of his vision, sometimes embracing her husband as if in sympathy.

One afternoon he heard a car rumbling up the driveway, an engine that sounded open to the air, ticking and knocking loudly. He recognized the rattle of the valves, the whir of an engine fan, the banging of pistons, the lively chug of exhaust coughing through a manifold. The engine stopped running and he could hear the sounds of squeaky leaf springs as someone stepped out of the car. The author walked to the window and looked down onto the driveway. The vehicle was one from his book, a roofless Spanish number from the mid-seventeenth century. Its tires were made of bull hide and its engine's components were forged and hammered at a special smithy outside of Toledo. It was entirely handmade—there was no other option back then. A man wearing strange spectacles, breeches, stockings, and pointed shoes was standing beside the car. He looked up at the author. *"Buenas tardes!"* he said, raising his be-feathered hat into the air, then bowing.

"Christ," the author said into the dark air of the bedroom.

Marvin called to his wife. "Sar', something's happening."

"Christ," the author said again as he watched the man walk toward the veranda, heard the front door open, the glass panes rattle. Then the hard footfalls moved along below him until they stopped at the bottom of the stairs. "Grandly entertaining," he said into the air again, his breathing labored.

Marvin leaned over his father.

Before long, the man with the cap came into the room and stopped at the foot of the bed.

"I ask that you look down at the vehicle again," the Spaniard said to the author, his voice gentle. *"Por favor, mira el vehículo de nuevo."*

The author went to the window again, cocked his head and did as requested. The ancient machine was quiet now, and sitting in the passenger's seat was Jennifer, his lovely wife, resembling the woman she'd been three decades ago.

"Hello stranger!" she said, looking up at him. "It's been ages. Are you going to join us?"

What a sight he must have made, he thought, a tormented and oafish face sprouting silver hair, corneas the color of skim milk.

"Do I have a choice in the matter?" he said.

She smiled, her teeth a little out of whack as always, her eyes bright blue, like gems.

"Such the reductionist," she said. "I'll be here. We'll go together."

"What's it like?" he said.

"As you've always suspected, it's nothing, nothing at all. Or, nothing*ness*."

He was on his back in bed again, his son and daughter-in-law standing on either side of him, each holding one of his hands. This was sweetness embodied, the warm human grip, his palm and fingers encased in the caresses of those who would inherit all of this from him. He could still see the Spaniard, who was now at the window looking down, nodding to Jennifer as if things were going swimmingly, the plumage of his absurd hat, which he held at his side, fluttering in the breeze. Oh, that air was wonderful. He would miss the scent of the trees! Typical, cliché, that that which you take for granted tugs at your heartstrings in the end.

Then the Spaniard turned toward him. "Are you ready to follow me? Please stand up and walk with me to the car. *Sí? Ponte de pie."*

A minute passed as the author considered the question.

"Frankly, this is bullshit," he finally said, having found his voice, having suddenly thought better of an expedited exit. He was in love with the air that came into the room, after all.

"No problemo. Haha, that's what people say, yes?" the Spaniard said. "We have patience. We can wait." Then he went to the window and gestured for Jennifer to join them. In a blink, she also stood at the foot of the bed, next to Marvin. Now the place was getting crowded, and the author was beginning to feel at home. Maybe he would stick around for a little while longer. Maybe he'd surprise them all.

Port Authority

PART I

I was waiting for the subway around midnight when I noticed this kid standing right next to me on the platform. He was in his late teens or early twenties, with acne scars and pencil-thin sideburns. He fidgeted, turned to look at me when I wasn't looking at him, and then looked away when I caught him doing it. Finally he turned to me and said, "What stop for the Port Authority Bus Terminal?"

"34th Street," I said. It came out reflexively. This was at the 8th Street stop in Manhattan and I was on my way to my job as a legal proofreader to work the graveyard shift. The problem was, I still hadn't recovered from an evening out with a couple of friends. My head was swimming.

"They don't only have Greyhound there, right?" he said. "They got all the other buses?"

"All the buses, that's right," I said.

I stepped back from the tracks when the R train pulled in, and we got on together. At the 28th Street stop I told the kid—the young man—that the next stop was his. "You'll have to walk a few blocks west underground. You don't even have to go outside." He didn't say anything to me, but he still seemed a little nervous when he got off.

About a second after the train doors closed, I realized I'd probably told him to get off at the wrong stop. Wasn't it clear as day that Port Authority was at 42nd Street, not 34th? In fact, yes, I'd given him the wrong directions. When I exited at 57th Street I checked a map on the station wall and there it was, where it has always been, on West 42nd Street.

I walked four blocks to the building where I work, took the elevator, booted up the computer, logged in, and, downing one cup of coffee after another, proofread legal contracts until the sun rose over Seventh Avenue.

A few nights later I was walking to my usual spot on the subway platform when I noticed that same kid standing there. I didn't want to deal with it and turned away, but he let loose one of those stadium whistles that stopped me in my tracks.

"I was going up to Detroit," he said. "My great-grandmother died. She was a hundred. One-hundred years old. Because of you I missed the service and almost missed the burial."

He was twenty feet away and shouting, moving toward me.

"Do I know you?" I said in feigned befuddlement.

I decided I should walk toward him as well so as not to seem cowed, and also to initiate some kind of mirror symmetry, which can be amusing with the right partner.

The few midnight commuters between us parted.

"Ah yes, now I remember. I sent you to the wrong stop. I was drunk," I said, smiling, as if this were the ultimate, inviolate excuse. "I should've sent you to 42nd, no?"

"I missed the bus and then I almost missed the burial."

"Got it," I said. "That's too bad."

"It doesn't matter. Not to my great-grandmother. She's dead, right?"

The hope of a brawl seemed to be getting some of our fellow travelers excited, and they were watching to see what happened next. Among them was a good-looking woman doctor, or doctor impersonator, wearing two stethoscopes around her pearly neck. Her blond hair was done up in a loose bun like an eighties porn star. Beyond her, a big guy done up in muddy construction worker garb looked shaken to the core, as if he'd been using a jackhammer for the last twenty-four hours. He was shooting what I'd call an invitation in my direction. His eyes were devoid of much in the way of affection, but I got his meaning. I had a feeling that if a fight broke out, he'd back me.

Then the misdirected kid got closer and looked at my face, like he could see something crawling on it. Okay, I thought, don't flinch—let him throw the first punch.

"Do you have dry skin?" he said.

"What?" I said.

"Your skin is flaking off your face. You need some moisturizer."

"I don't know," I said.

"I can get you some high-grade moisturizer from a top US firm," he said.

"Like I said, I'm sorry about the misunderstanding."

"How much do you pay for toothpaste?" the kid asked.

Christ, I thought, he's sort of a genius for turning this around so quickly. Here I was worried that I'd have to fight for the first time in a long time, and here he was commercially capitalizing on that fear and vulnerability. A real American. I knew where this was heading.

"I'm not interested in Amway," I said.

"This is *not* Amway."

I walked away and got on the first car when the train came.

The last thing I heard him say was, "Pets?"

A week later he was standing at that same spot again, wearing tri-colored alligator skin shoes, designer jeans, and a houndstooth sports jacket under which a tight-fitting mock turtleneck showed he had some pecs. His skin looked good. The acne scars had faded to almost nothing at all. His hair, black and lustrous, was thick and started low on his forehead at a little widow's peak.

At his side was a petite woman with long straight black hair and bangs who, in turn, had a sort of extra-dimensional, brightly-hued cart-on-wheels by *her* side. He saw me from a distance, whispered something to her, and she locked the wheels on the cart with her foot. She opened some of the drawers and inspected their contents with faked interest as I headed past them to my usual spot. The subway pulled in almost immediately and I, hoping to escape, was about to step on when the kid placed a hand on each of my shoulders and eased me back.

"I've got something to show you," he said.

The train door closed an inch from my face.

"Your skin may not be that bad after all," he shouted over the diminishing din of the train, "but what Michiko and I are sensing is that your attitude is all wrong. We don't have anything for that, per se. Nothing topical, that is. But we do have—"

"I'm not interested," I interrupted.

"What we do have are intelligent nanotubes."

He motioned to Michiko, who adroitly drew forth from one of the more brightly luminescing drawers of her cart a cylinder with a cork in one end. She removed the cork with her incisors and handed the cylinder to her partner.

"We're administering them on a test basis, *gratis*," he said.

"I have to get to work," I said, "And now I've got to wait for another goddamned train."

"These," he said, holding up the vial, "are straight from Murray Hill, New Joisey. Fell off the back of an electron microscope. Know what's in Murray Hill, New Joisey?"

I turned and began walking to the other end of the platform, which seemed to be continually extending out into the subway tunnel at the same pace at which I progressed.

"Bell Laboratories," I heard the kid shout in answer to his own question.

Michiko was soon walking behind me in her flats. She asked me to please stop for one moment so she could say something. The exit sign was a few yards ahead. I should have kept going.

"Just turn, please, to show that you are a gentleman," she said.

I turned.

She lifted an atomizer and misted me in the face.

I was on my back on a station bench and a young woman leaned over me, her t-shirt brushing against my face. She smelled like cigarettes, alcohol, and something sepulchral. Her pants were speckled with beet and carrot juice. I looked at her groin and her thick military belt that missed every other loop, at her low-riders that she wore too low, at her little roll of a belly and flattened navel, at the head of a snake tattoo peeking up from her pubis.

"Oh, you're *up*," she said.

She was looking in the direction of my feet with her hand deep in my inside jacket pocket.

"Take it easy, mister. I was looking for your ID. ``

My mouth was filled with bile and grit. My bowels felt like they'd been violated. I held her arm.

"You're beginning to hurt me." She spoke with a British accent.

"Nanotubes," I said. "They put them inside me."

"Please let go of me," she said.

She unhooked her cell phone from a thin wire that ran down the front of her pants. She was still for a moment, looking at me with either suspicion or pity. Her irises were variegated blue and green. The blue was grayish; the green was bluish.

"I can call 911. You need to go to hospital."

" '*The*,' " I said, "and nonsense. Help me up."

Her short dark hair had a magenta streak, and she wore ironic, garish eyeliner. That navel of hers was opening and closing as she moved around, frowning and smiling, making O's as if astonished with the world. Oh shit, did I ever feel like crap. I looked down. My belt was hitched, but on a looser setting than usual. I now felt certain that things were crawling around inside of me, from the mouth down, from the rectum up.

What would happen when they met?

When I got back up to my apartment I called in sick to Joel, who runs my shift at the law firm. He's an opera singer by day and gets a decent number of off-Broadway gigs that don't pay the bills. Then I went to the bathroom and ended up jamming the toilet so that I had to take the plunger to it. I laughed. My damn bowels are such good harbingers of my emotional state of affairs that I can tell when a fit of depression is coming on because I defecate like a marmoset. But tonight I was obviously feeling magnanimous, open to possibilities, a real go-getter. Intelligent nanotubes or not, I thought, let me see what this night yields.

How can I explain the spell that came over me, that drove my actions? Minute by minute I was in control—true. Yet behind it all an end game had been imprinted upon some gauzily obscured level of my consciousness, an end game to which I could not gain access. It was as if some glue-sniffing bloke had hotwired my soul and was behind the controls of my mind.

I ironed an Egyptian cotton shirt, showered, and decided I should feed the cats, who seemed agitated and were nipping at my ankles for attention. "What?" I asked them after they ignored the freshly presented wet food. "What?" But the cats' following me around had apparently not indicated what it normally had—that they were hungry. The two of them looked at me with wide eyes and filled the air with high-pitched mews for some other reason. But what was it? That feline perceptions clearly trump human ones was a worry; that sporadically throughout the ages these little furry beasts had been thought to be in league with the devil or other pagan and dark forces only added to my concern. I love them, naturally, but could they sense in me something deathly or evil, half-monster, bitter-smelling, despairing?

I looked at myself in the person-sized mirror. I looked okay. Nothing special. Standard skinny but solid-built guy, average height, curly hair sprouting from his shoulders, beard about ten percent gray. My pupils, on close inspection, were fully dilated, which was unusual.

On the other side of the apartment I could hear one of the cats digging in its litter box.

I felt clean inside and out, sharp, no clouds of doubt obscuring my thoughts. Look into your own eyes, I commanded myself, and leaned forward. A planet in each one. But deeper, inside my mind, there were not many thoughts at all. I wanted. I wanted. I wanted something. Nothing but an odd emptiness resided within me, I had to admit. A desirous sort of *something*. In particle physics it might have been the manifestation of an undiscovered particle whose near speed-of-light collision gives rise to paradoxes thus far unimagined. Anti-space folded within lust, wrapped in layers of longing.

Then something more disturbing happened, a brief dash of an event that I'm embarrassed to pass along. I'd recently switched the cats over to a fancy sort of food because I'd gotten a two-thousand dollar per year raise and thought, why not share the wealth? For the last week I'd been feeding them things like Organic Lamb Stew and Hearty Halibut and the like. The problem was that in my disturbed state the fresh turds my cat had released into the litter smelled good. I mean they smelled edible in a pungent way, like corned beef hash frying in a cast iron skillet. I immediately recognized that something was awry, that a short circuit had occurred, some tripped up crossover from my olfactory center into my food imaging center. I cut off the urge to actually take a fork and stick it in the shit, but it was too late to stop the desire to eat something as odoriferous as high-class cat turds. I looked in the fridge and cupboards, and the only thing that struck my fancy was a little can of expensive tapenade, which I opened and began eating with the two-finger scoop.

I opened my window and stuck my head outside. It had been drizzling for days and the streets, though essentially quiet so late at night, gave echo to footsteps and the occasional taxi spinning out on the wet asphalt. I was going out there, into the night, revved up, feeling some large and ever-expanding emptiness inside of me that needed filling. An emptiness with mass, a paradoxical space, a ravenous desire that was both armless and legless. I was being driven by the bloke, and where he'd take me I wasn't sure.

Smile. Head on out.

Part II

I stood facing the brownstone on East 12th Street close to Fifth Avenue and gazed in through the large windows, through the diaphanous curtains. I saw the silhouettes of people holding drinks—the dying embers of a party:

couples and throuples ensconced in booze and comfort, biding their time before they moved on to the next untoward phase of the night. I saw them through sixteen-over-sixteen double-sash bay windows framed by ornate exterior woodwork, woodwork I'd watched get restored over the last several months by a single craftsman from another era—an older Black man in overalls whose scaffolding and lockbox were finally gone. I must have walked past this brownstone hundreds of times over the course of the last decade, but had wondered about its occupants only vaguely. Until now.

The front sitting room looked like a real beauty from the street—the chandelier's shimmering crystal, the dark wainscoting, the antique birdcage with a stuffed parrot—a child's toy—on its perch placed front and center for all those on the sidewalk to see. How humorous! These people were grand. I stood motionless, watched, and tried to find something to play with in my pocket until suddenly, in a flash, I realized I was to enter the building.

Whence did this inspiration spring? At the semantic level, it seemed, since the thought came to me fully formed, as if it were the last chain in a logical progression of smaller thoughts, but these thoughts were nowhere to be found.

A woman leaving the party through the front door allowed me into the foyer. A young man, well-dressed and exhaling pot smoke, let me pass from the foyer into the apartment proper. From there I made a quick right and was in the sitting room I had been admiring outwardly.

Empty tumblers and stemware were grouped on a few tables, on a pair of big stereo speakers, on a sideboard. Ice, melted and rounded, floated in some. A cigar with an inch of ashes smoldered in a brass ashtray. Hello everyone! Nobody was in the room. They were gathering jackets and hats and capes in a side room as they left. They were out of view but I could hear the soft tones of their comfortable voices. The foyer door and, with more muffle, the door to the street, kept opening and closing as guests left. And look at these sofas! Stuffed to the hilt; brown, worn leather with discrete fissures on the surface like veins in marble.

Then I heard a female voice say, "And you would be?"

I turned and there stood a woman a decade or more my senior, taller than me, dressed in embroidered jeans and a silk t-shirt, nice face, relaxed and pleasant looking. WASPy, but not aggressively. Not merely blond hair, but blond features—angular jaw, pert nose, eyes that should have been blue, and may have been. She held a sprig of celery between her fingers like a cigarette.

"Are you Robert's friend?"

"Yes," I said, "that's right."

"From the Woodward?"

"The Woodward."

Why not.

"Robert always retreats to his books after a nice party. Tries to give our guests the hint. 'Time to go,' you know."

"When it's time, it's time," I said.

"Did you bring the package?"

"The package. . . from the Woodward?"

"Presumably from you, Mr. —? Was Robert supposed to have given me your name? I'm sure he did but I've forgotten. I'm a shit like that. Please do introduce yourself."

"Thompson, Gene."

"Well then we share a name, Mr. Thompson. Jean Alcross, drunken." She extended her hand—dry, supple, warm—and I took it. "Please, catch up with some drinks and then we'll see what happens."

She steered me into the kitchen, where the help—two women and a man, dressed in white top to bottom—had sorted out the empty bottles and were wiping down those that still had some liquor in them. The white rags they were using looked cleaner than most of my undershirts.

"Go on," Jean Alcross said, "pick your poison."

I poured myself something from a stoneware bottle.

"That's apple brandy from Normandy," Jean said.

"Calvados," I said.

"You know your liquor, Gene," she said.

She walked me back into the living room. A few guests were still leaving and she went to attend to them. I sat on one of those overstuffed couches and got a closer look at the toy bird in its antique birdcage. In a few minutes Jean Alcross stuck her head in.

"I'm going to let Robert know you're here. I don't know if he'll see you."

She said it in the nicest possible way.

What he was expecting—what I was expecting—was a mystery. Somewhere deep inside I was scared. On the other hand, the smell of the old leather, the apple brandy, the fading odor of canapés and ripe cheeses were all acting to get me a little over-stimulated.

And I found myself meditating on Jean Alcross. She looked like a runner, a sprinter or hurdler as opposed to the stick figure marathoners I'd met—all sinew and arteries. Alcross had nice arms and small breasts. Her legs were shapely and muscular in those blue jeans. Great color in her face. Some gray hairs, and she had calm eyes. The color of. . . well I still don't know what. I can't remember the color of her eyes, only their effect. Everything was under her control and always would be, those eyes said.

By the time she inserted herself into my line of vision again my tumbler was empty and I'd nicely lain myself out on the sofa.

"My husband would like to see you. He wants to know if you've got the package?"

"Right here," I said, patting one of my empty pockets.

"Oh, I didn't realize it was so small."

She led me up the steps, her buttocks spelling out all kinds of words as they undulated before me. Two flights up, then three, then four. I'd broken into a sweat. She stopped before we got to the last landing.

"He's taken over the whole top floor with his studies. Let yourself through those doors. And if you'd be kind enough to tell him I'm going to bed, I'd be grateful."

A pair of French doors with brass knobs awaited me at the top of the steps. I opened them.

Robert Alcross was illuminated by a half-dozen antique-y incandescent bulbs, the kind where the glass is clear and the filaments resemble uvulas. They provided the retro effect he wanted—I'm sure of that. He was an odd one, I could tell straight off the bat. Books were all over the place: atlases, encyclopedias and codexes, stapled pamphlets filled with geometrical diagrams. I didn't take more than a few steps into the space.

"Well well, the messenger has arrived. In the guise of, is it Mr. Thompson?" Robert Alcross said, sliding across the room on his desk chair. "I expected someone less. . . petite. More robust." He eyed me up and down.

"Gene's the name."

"Sure it is. I'm correct in calling you Mr. Schmidt?"

"No. It's Gene Thompson."

"Just keep insisting, Mr. Schmidt."

"Gene Thompson."

"Laramie Mist sounds better. I'm in favor of more creative faux names," He rose and moved toward me with two or three elastic strides.

"Gene Thompson's the name."

"Loretto DiGiovano?"

"Gene Thompson."

"Farty Tabernacle?"

"I believe I might have made a mistake," I finally said. "I thought that I had business here."

"What kind of business?"

"Well—I'm not sure."

"You came into my home without knowing why?"

"Afraid so."

"What drove you here?"

"I had this. . . " It was no use, I thought. "I had this feeling that I should come here. A feeling I don't know how to explain." I was beginning to get angry as I homed in on the truth of the attack. "I was guided here somehow. After a dose of. . . oh never mind."

"Dosed by whom?"

"By what, you mean. What do you do, exactly, Robert?"

"I'm a researcher of sorts. You could call me an explorer of a kind."

"Of what kind?"

"Of realms."

"Realms? Do you happen to know a kid with funny sideburns, about eighteen years old, and a girl named Michiko?"

"I can't recall."

"Something that kid and the girl did, a violation of dignity—something they put inside of me. . . "

My memory was full of holes along the edges. But why not push things, get this guy to talk? I was having a good time. My blood was racing, I could hear nothing else in my ears.

"Something they did to me also made me not care what I do to you. Or your wife. She's a looker. A little giraffy, but a looker." I would have never said these words, yet the voice was mine. "By the way, she wanted me to tell you that she's gone to bed. I could use my nose to figure out where the bedroom is."

And then, well I didn't plan on this. I grabbed his trachea. High school self-defense classes, one after the other. A nonviolent kid, I was bored stiff and sometimes bullied back in the day. And now it came into my fingers that they might as well do their stuff, since I had been bullied into coming to this fancy garret. My right hand gripped Robert Alcross's trachea like a plumber's wrench grips a corroded fitting.

"Tell me what's up," I said.

He began to change color, though he remained calm, as if he knew that deep down I wouldn't actually kill him. His glasses began to slip forward on his nose and for some reason this did it to me, made him look too vulnerable for my liking. I let him go.

"Side effects," he said, regaining his breath. "Aggression," pause, "increased sexual tension," pause, "heightened olfactory sensitivity. That's a new one. You say you can smell my wife? You dog," and he laughed, rubbing his neck. Then he lowered the lights as if to calm a panicked animal. "You've been infused. Most likely you have a sense that this has occurred. The smallest of suppositories is all our good friends administered. We really would have preferred your acquiescence. The nanotubes are working in concert now, I can see. They have coalesced to send you the most fundamental of commands—to arrive at our modest home. In a few hours you'll be your old self again, banal as ever, and *nice*."

I considered grabbing his trachea again for old times' sake, could see the imprints my fingers had already made. I was feeling obsessive enough to match them exactly. But he stepped back and reached into his breast pocket and withdrew a fob, a small ellipsoid with one button.

"I don't work without patient disincentives. You carry not only my nanotubes, but the ingredients of a grave poison. If I press this button," he said, "a powerful neurotoxin normally produced by *Clostridium botulinum* will be released into your bloodstream. You'll come down with a respectable case of botulism. Cause of death: suffocation due to paralysis of the diaphragm. So, don't fuck with me."

I reached for the fob but he hovered his thumb over the button.

"Why me?" I said.

"Ah yes, the age-old question. It's not as if you've won the lottery. But I am glad you asked. You see your work routine is one of mundanity and repetition—an excruciating repetition of actions and thoughts to no real end. This has etched wide unencumbered highways into your neural network, vast and beautiful spaces that lack complexity and interference of any kind. Our process uses these pathways to accrete nanotubes into what might be called notions or impulses. And while nobody is expendable—and please don't think we have any intent of harming you—those who work the night shift performing the task of legal proofreading generally have far less utility than day workers who draft the documents in the first place, if you get my drift. Meaning if things were to go awry, societal damage is minimized. And yes, don't worry, we'd take care of your cats, find them a home that provided affection. If there's one thing I abhor, it's animal cruelty." He took his glasses off and placed the fob on a countertop, and then he stepped toward me.

"I can't tell you how thrilled I am to have you standing here. It's an odd thing to say, but. . . may I shake your hand? You're the first success I've had—my first real success! Just look at you."

I must admit that I was getting excited myself, and I'm still under the notion that these were my own thoughts, not purposeful, pre-packaged junk thoughts injected into my vast unencumbered neural highways. Truth is, I'll never know.

I took the man's hand firmly and shook it with sincerity and love.

Why, you might ask, would I be happy to be there? For one—and this is not to be minimized—I was tripping. Whatever these accreting nanotubes were doing, they were suddenly making me feel as if the world were a pulsing breast from which I had suckled for all these years, ungrateful for the life it had given me—until now. This fellow woke me up after a lifetime of unenlightened drift. Also, I felt enwrapped by the warmth of the air in the uvula-lit garret, and here I admit it was mostly because these people were rich and I was not, and the wealthy always make me feel obsequious and oh-so humble to be in their presence (and they also don't skimp on heat). Simultaneously, I felt prone to violence, able to tear a human being limb from limb or make love with beautiful, illegal destruction. At that moment it didn't seem that my keeper fully understood these inklings of superhumanness. If he did, he seemed awfully relaxed about the whole thing.

I couldn't imagine going back to my normal routine, to that tired pull of gravity, my achy sinuses, the incessant need to be loved by my ridiculous felines and even more ridiculous family and friends—to the endless want of affection in all its nasty variations. No, I'd stay here and admire the ropey veins now rising on the back of my hands, do a handstand to the triumphal music that was playing in my head. You see my psyche was collapsing upon itself with exponential haste. Soon I would be but an emotional singularity pulsing in the rarefied night.

He took me by the hand, actually by the bitty tips of my fingers, and as if by a spell steered me into a room lit by a hundred candles where Barry Manilow was playing quietly out of some ceiling speakers. Jean Alcross was in bed already, naked above the waist, the blankets pulled down to her hips. The shadows her little round breasts cast over the rest of her danced with each candle flicker.

"What's this all about?" I pretended to be surprised.

"You want to see more?" She smiled with an open mouth. Then she threw the blanket off. All the while, as I stood there taking in her lanky body that shone brightly with healthy skin and 100% depilation, her husband was giving me a back rub. Then he was sliding his soft, unworked fingers beneath my shirt color, tickling the wool-like hair on the back of my neck. Then he was whispering confidence-boosting mantras into my ear from behind while simultaneously unbuttoning my shirt.

"You're a man's man; you know what makes the world spin; when you bat, you always hit a homer; the world follows your lead; your body is to die for. . . " All the while he was gently pushing me down and toward his wife. "Go to her," he finally said. Her arms were open to me, her regal smile promising the world.

What I remember most as the morning sun came in through the windows was Robert Alcross making cappuccino on the other side of the room, his rhythmic foaming of the milk, the pitch getting lower as the froth built. This had always been a purely retail-chain sound to me, the racket of Starbucks or other tattooed-barista joints in which I had no business spending anything over two dollars, for I was strictly a drip man.

Yet he was making the coffee for me and his wife, who was now leaning on one elbow and sniffing me with a smile, the perfumed soles of her feet brushing against my chin. That's when I realized that that's what this had all been about in the end—bringing home a pair of roses for the missus.

Robert Alcross, grinning at the scene from across the room, was wearing bespoke tweeds and shoes that cost as much as a Ford Fiesta. He was a man whose day-old scruff looked as if it were terrified at having emerged from his well-oiled follicles into the morning light. From the angle of the sun, I guessed it must have been close to 8:00 a.m., and he was dressed for work, whatever that entailed.

Beta

Cheryl Warren was sprawled out on the pleather sofa, deep into a fashion magazine made thick with perfume inserts. George, who was peering out their large picture window watching the sun set over the Palisades, heard the crinkling sound of a page turning, and awaited the next olfactory ad. A rock slide two months ago had left a fresh gash in the façade across the Hudson, the traprock slough having utterly crushed hundreds of trees along with a lone hiker whose body parts were still being recovered. If you're dead-set against subtlety, George thought, then it's not a bad way to go. He wondered if the poor chum had managed a few seconds of decent self-reflection before the cliff came down on him.

"Next week this time and she'll be back," came the voice from behind him. "I can see the worry on your face. Don't deny it."

"I'm not denying it," he said.

Their daughter was camping with a group of friends on Mt. Desert Island in Maine, some five-hundred miles distant from the cozy Yonkers condo in which she'd spent the majority of her life. Though Sandra was just past eighteen years old, she and her friends had no supervision and were out of cellphone range, at the mercy of those stony beaches, towering pines, and wily park rangers. Yet their daughter's little adventure did not seem to bother Cheryl, who by her nature was blindly optimistic, a courted focus group participant. But possibly his wife did not understand that George did not actually fear for his daughter's safety—he knew she would be fine. What bothered him was the *idea of it all.*

"Two full weeks," he said. "She's perfectly happy to shut us out for two full weeks."

"That's as it should be," Cheryl said. "You do want an independent daughter, right?"

He nodded.

"Well then."

"And she's out of here starting next month," he said, knowing that this was contributing to a sudden hollowness in his chest: Sandra's pending departure for college, her exit from their local lives. He turned to see that his wife hadn't diverted her attention from the scented magazine.

"Oneonta is not exactly the far-flung reaches of the planet," she said, turning another page. A subscription postcard fell out and landed on her chest. She let it lie there, a rigid paper rectangle upon her large cockeyed breasts that looked at opposite ends of the room, that made taut the fabric of her Lycra T-shirt. No comment, George thought, cognizant of his body's own migration toward the Earth's hilarious molten core.

Finally, she turned to look at him. "It's sweet that you miss her before she's even packed up. You do know that, right?"

That night in bed, he curled into Cheryl from behind, pressing himself into the back of her thigh. Was a time when this gentle prodding would get her to throw off the blankets and raise her backside into the air for him. But now she merely reached behind and ran her hand up his soft, fur-lined belly, turned to face him, and gave him a nice slow kiss on the lips.

"I'm fading, baby, I'm fading," she said, a little salivary snap as she smiled, her eyes closing, the smell of wine and organic deodorant rising up from beneath the covers. And yet she moved her hand back down and fell asleep holding his erection, which remained at attention well after all hope had been lost. At last it wilted in her hand. That's the way it had been, intermittently, for the last year or so. It seemed to George that his prick had become her soporific charm. Soon she was breathing through her nose with a bit of a whistle. Her hair, lustrous black streaked with gray, covered her eyes. How many times had he seen her in that exact position, lit greenly by their nightstand clock? A thousand, two-?

The central air conditioning pushed freezing, mildewy air into the bedroom. He couldn't stand it—they might as well be in a capsule hurtling across the galaxy. Though it had passed only recently, he longed for the return of spring, when the system pulled in the floral essence from plantings by the main intake grill. And how sad is that? he thought. You yearn for a season as delivered through duct work.

At last he began to settle into position for the night, his heart booming away, his eyelids becoming heavy, his wife's breathing a hypnotic and familiar backbeat. And then he was soundly asleep. He awoke in the same position, diffuse sunlight coming through the bedroom blinds. His left forearm and hand were completely numb, Cheryl having rolled onto the crook of his elbow in the night.

"Babe?" he said, pulling the dead arm out from under her. "Wow," and he held the forearm in his opposite hand, contemplating its heft—his own inert matter—in a manner only special times like this afforded. He shimmied out of bed, dragging the dead thing with him. It was 6:30 a.m. and he put on the coffee machine.

God, he thought, or an approximation thereof, awaited him.

The Consortium's northeast regional headquarters was housed in a converted General Motors factory in North Tarrytown. The Consortium's major (some said only) project was an effort that had taken almost five years to build and was now on the verge of public release. It was called the Multivariate Predictive Engine, known internally as the MPE, the Engine, or the Fucking Beast. That morning, George attended the biweekly "open voice" meeting, a forum during which engineers and designers could ask questions of each other and of any product managers who'd deigned to show. Questions that nobody could satisfactorily answer would be escalated to the Operations Committee.

"Are we simply trying to get answers to difficult questions in under four-hundred milliseconds," asked a young woman George had never seen before, likely a recent grad who'd beat out the competition, "or are we doing something much more? Because to me it feels like we're creating some sort of an emulator. . . a God emulator, to be frank." A tall, frail-looking, and extremely pale Asian-American, she stood her ground as those present—mostly white men—turned to stare at her. George believed her to be one of the code compliance officers, charged with ensuring that engineers followed internationally accepted programming standards that guaranteed a semblance of stability. "To be honest it seems, like, a little crazy?" she said.

"An emulator is pushing it, don't you think?" said George, volunteering a response before he knew what he was doing. "To imply the MPE is anything even approaching a deity would be disingenuous, and, agreed, crazy-sounding if word were to get out. Believe me, we have no intent of setting up a direct line to the big guy in the sky." Some of his colleagues chuckled. They always seemed uncomfortable.

"Adding to George's sentiment, I'll say that we've been through this discussion a hundred times before, before our new colleague arrived." This was Les McClutchy, one of the database guys and a real devotee to the project. He was fiftyish, athletic, and always sported an injury of one kind or another. Today he was wearing a butterfly bandage beneath his left eye, as if he'd been boxing. "And yet," he added, raising a taped finger, "if there is a hidden structure to things—a unifying voice that every physicist, mathematician, philosopher and poet has missed over the last twenty-five centuries, the Engine will be there to extract its proclamations."

"Actually, I don't buy that it's that simple," the woman said, her lips pinched with agitation. This was clearly not easy for her. She hadn't yet drunk the Kool-Aid. Suspicion and doubt still had its talons in her. "I'm on board, don't get me wrong," she said, holding up one hand prophylactically, "but I'm saying, I'm saying, it's crazy?" and she trailed off, losing her wherewithal.

Yes, crazy indeed, George thought. It was no small effort to illuminate the inner workings of that temporal system we call reality. And yet this young woman, a freshly minted computer science major recruited from Stanford or MIT, had caught his attention with her panic-stricken intelligence, her inquisitions no match for corporate momentum. The paint was barely dry on the three data centers—in Poughkeepsie, Toulouse, and Acequia, Idaho—that hosted the Engine's vast corpus of data, and yet everyone was coiled, wet of mouth, ready to flip the switch to ON. George and his team had built the user interface, the portal by which the curious hordes would enter their queries and only moments later be delighted by the precise answers they'd receive, always grammatically correct with never a hint of sarcasm or irony.

The invention engendered a number of inherent dangers. For example, the Operations Committee was dead set against users asking the Engine how a specific stock would perform, or at least an answer being returned. George, on the other hand, thought it would be fine. Why not let the Fucking Beast act as the great economic equalizer, the killer of arbitrage? No inefficiencies to exploit means Wall Street goes poof.

He did wonder what would happen if people took the merely probabilistic answers as truth—or even as sacred. What then? In the most volatile cases, wouldn't the answers drive the outcome? Could the world become a crazy quilt of self-fulfilling prophecies?

Whatever happened, one thing George knew for sure: in a couple of months, tops, everyone on the planet would be tapping his buttons and fingering his menus on their shiny little screens.

His glass-walled office was on the second floor and, like his home, overlooked the Hudson River. The building's central mezzanine rose from the main lobby to the roof, five stories above, where a mosaic of skylights resembling hubcaps let lazy light filter in. Offices like George's ringed the interior of the building and were accessed by either a series of open-air stairways or by two glass elevators, one on either end of the building. At around noon, George leaned over the railing outside of his office and looked down at the ground floor, at the grid of low-walled cubicles, the engineers and quality assurance people with their diagrams and white boards and double monitors where, decades earlier, Corvettes had rolled down the line.

As he looked out over the floor, a bolt of proactivism hit him: he was thinking that he'd like to do more, that he could join one of the Quality Assurance teams and help them test queries, get his hands a little dirty with more of the back-end stuff, bang away at some good ol' C++ if they'd let him. He'd even volunteer for a stint at the datacenter in Poughkeepsie—work the computer racks, replace dead processors and cooling fans, cut his knuckles on server boxes.

He raised his eyes and looked across the open expanse to the office opposite his. One of the Orthodox Jewish engineers was *davening* at his desk. George wasn't Jewish, had nothing against the Jewish people. Religion in general—serious, humorless, eye-for-an-eye religion—frightened the hell out of him, no matter its denomination or sect. Sending complex queries into the vast computational universe: that didn't seem profound when he thought about it as merely a bunch of algorithms and APIs chugging along and doing their things. But when he saw this bearded fellow, a man who'd built his life around the Torah and the Talmud, and when he thought about what this project was supposed to mean to him—that was too much to take in. For this man, this was *it*, a trumping of all inherent mysteries, a hopeful conjuring of the messiah.

The man stopped praying as three of his skullcapped colleagues climbed the perforated steel steps to the catwalk. They entered his glass-walled office single file, one of them carrying a stack of pre-packaged kosher lunches. The four laid out their meals and utensils but before long were on their feet whiteboarding equations, diagramming server clusters. A heated discussion ensued, with much gesticulating, followed by a rapid-fire erasing and re-drawing of switches and pathways. Watching the men made George agitated and hungry.

Doris Amelia, his officemate, sat in the far corner of their shared cell, her back to him, her large monitor displaying several graphs. They measured latency, CPU usage, queries-per-second, and other real-time metrics related to back-end processes. She would be the first to know if any machines went offline in Toulouse or Poughkeepsie, if a broken pipe error was gumming up the dataworks in Acequia. She was fifty-three, a new grandmother, and had festooned the corner above her desk with photos of an infant girl so small that the images were slightly blurry.

Cheryl had packed for George a hummus sandwich on pita bread along with a pear and oatmeal cookies. When she made a batch of hummus their apartment was alive with frenzy, the food processor jumping as it ground the chickpeas, concretions of tahini sticking to rubber spatulas, the scent of garlic and lemon juice tingling his nostrils. He smiled at the recollection of this drama and unwrapped his sandwich with some domestic tenderness. He took a bite. The hummus was still a little cool from their refrigerator.

Then his cellphone began vibrating on his desk.

"Baby," he said, the hummus slowing his speech, "Good timing. I'm eating your magic sandwich–"

"Sandra's going to be okay," came his wife's voice, shaky and stumbling, "but there's been a car accident, a terrible accident. I'm on my way to Grand Central right now to come home."

George swallowed, put the sandwich down.

"A logging truck hit their car," his wife continued, breathing hard. She must have been huffing it on foot. "One of the boys they were with. . . he was killed instantly. Sandra's leg is fractured and she needed some stitches on her face, but she's going to be okay George, she's going to be fine, thank God. We need to drive up to Maine—to Bangor—and fetch her."

"Please say again," George said from within an envelope of disbelief.

"I said that our daughter has a fractured leg and some kind of laceration on her face. The dead boy, his name is Johnny Delano. Do you remember him? I don't. I think they'd just begun dating. What a way to get started in love."

When the call was over, he turned to find Doris Amelia standing in the middle of the office, facing him. "George?" she said.

He thought back to the morning, to his dead forearm, the way he'd felt its mass, its dumb heft. His entire body now felt lifeless, nearly two-hundred pounds of inert matter pushing down stupidly into his chair. Somewhere in the midst of this sack of viscera his heart was supposedly keeping things going.

"George?" Doris Amelia said again. He'd never noticed how powerfully built she was, this purposeful dark-skinned woman "from the islands," as she liked to classify herself, wearing blue jeans and no-brand flats, a cotton sweater of an unfamiliar color hanging off her broad shoulders.

"My daughter's going to be okay, but she's got a fractured leg," and he repeated the news about the boy. (He wasn't sure he'd ever met this Johnny Delano. Was he the young man with the pierced lip that wore all the rings? Or the blonde boy, the one from Connecticut that she'd brought to the family's holiday party?) "We have to fetch her in Maine," George said. "It's Tuesday? I'll be back Thursday or Friday." He was regaining his composure now, and rose from his chair, his legs a little rubbery. "People can call my cell for emergencies."

An hour later they were driving the ancient Saab on the Cross County Parkway, the car's nose pointed northeast.

The Bangor weather had turned cold and rainy, and the sun was well down when they arrived at the hospital. Sandra was sedated and sleeping in a shared room with a dividing curtain, her face half covered in gauze and a little bit swollen. But she seemed at peace, snoozing with that expression that George had always interpreted as an inward smile, as if her ridiculous hopefulness—a quality most definitely not inherited from her father—could not help but manifest itself, even in sleep. They couldn't check her out until morning, so he and Cheryl took a room at a roadside motel a few blocks away.

"We've been spared. Is it bad to toast to our good luck?" George said, passing the bottle of cheap red they'd picked up along the boulevard. They were sitting cross-legged on the dingy carpet and leaning against the bed.

"Considering the circumstances, definitely," and she took a swig.

The beginning of the ride home was mostly silent. Sandra, on some heavy painkillers and sitting in the back seat lengthwise because of her cast, wept now and then, but that was it. The wound on her face had required five stitches and was now covered with a small child's bandage—pink hearts and butterflies—low on her cheek.

"We were in love, we were," she said without warning, two hours in.

Driving, George nodded his head, made eye contact with his daughter through the rearview mirror. He dared not ask who this Johnny Delano was—the blonde kid or the other one. Nor could he tell whether those dark circles under her eyes were artifacts of a broken heart or of the car accident itself. Not that it mattered which. It was a package deal—either way the poor girl was beaten down. For the first time she looked like an adult, an unnerved one.

Finally, many hours later, as they lumbered past Hartford and its insurance towers, she seemed to emerge from her funk.

"Dad, how's the job?"

"You know, it's work."

"Yeah, I do know that. I mean, do you think you'll be able to talk to God?"

"It's complicated."

She had a good memory; he'd give her that. Back in the early days of the project, well over two years ago, he'd joked that they would be "building the world's first omniscient deity." But he'd since lost his evangelism and cringed that he'd ever spoken like that. At a minimum, it could get him in trouble.

"Of course it's complicated. Be concise, Dad. That's part of your job, right?"

"What I mean to say is, I've got my doubts about the Engine, about its long-term viability as a useful force in our society."

"Fine. But can we try? I want to see if I can find out about Johnny. I want to see if I can find out why God, fate, or stupid fickle chance would let this happen. Don't you see, Johnny was am-a-zing. He wouldn't hurt a fly. He was a vegan, for crying out loud." Aha, George thought, it was the boy with all the piercings, all the rings. He was skinny, pore-less, a good smile, now that he thought about it. "And I want to see how he's doing up there in heaven. You know, in the whatever-comes-next."

"Sandra, I can't even imagine how terrible it must feel," George said. "That kind of loss when you're starting off. I've never been through it, and neither has your mother."

"I want to say again how sorry I am, honey," Cheryl said. "Luckily you're young enough for a second chance at love, even a third and fourth, as many as you need."

"Dad, can we try?" Sandra said.

"Since when are you interested in my job? And haven't I been clear? It's not a deity; it's a multivariate correlator. You understand the difference? I don't think you'll get much information about where Johnny is now. We should have tried a good robust query about the safety of your route before you left. That might have helped."

"Great, thanks so much for that," Sandra said, and started to cry.

"Well done, George," his wife said.

Back home at the condo, Cheryl made a pot of mint tea and the three of them stood around the kitchen counter watching it steep, not sure of what to say. Then George turned and hugged his daughter, kissed the white part in her hair. She embraced him back. Behind her on the kitchen counter he could see the camera he'd bought her for the camping trip, the housing and screen now cracked, its seams filled with dried blood.

"So," Sandra said into her father's shoulder, "can we?"

"Can we what?"

"The Engine. I want to use it."

"Honey, it's not feasible right now." Not exactly true, but he didn't want to explain the dangers of running untested code, the insane political risk he'd have to take to let an outsider—even his own daughter—try it. He knew he shouldn't even be contemplating it, yet this was his own flesh and blood. . . his injured baby.

She hugged him harder, this strong daughter of his, her upper arms grasping his chest as if trying to squeeze the air out of him.

"Are you sure?" she said into his neck. He could feel her chest spasm as she held back her tears.

"Yes, Sandra, yes. I'm sorry."

"I love you anyway." She released him, grabbed her crutches, and tripod-ed into her room, closing the door.

"Honey," Cheryl shouted, "the tea will be ready in a minute."

She turned to her husband. "Maybe letting her use that thing will help her mourn."

"It can't. She doesn't seem to get it. Anyway, give it a little time and she'll forget she even asked."

On a Sunday afternoon two weeks later, George drove north on Route 9 toward his place of employment. His daughter sat beside him, the passenger seat pushed all the way back for her cast.

"No guarantees," he said.

"You've said that like a hundred times. I understand. And thank you in advance."

"And it doesn't do well with the metaphysical, the existential." He could never get the difference between the two straight in his mind.

Soon he and Sandra were in his glass-walled office, the old factory empty but for a few engineers milling around on the first floor, and another pair playing ping pong off in the rec room, the sound of which infiltrated the place like a timid heartbeat.

He booted up his computer, signed into the test servers and, after surveying the adjacent offices and taking a deep breath, deployed the newest build of code. The instinct that drove him was love, and he could only hope this exercise would bring his daughter some comfort and peace. Before long the user interface (in beta) was displayed, with its big text box, blinking cursor, and *Ask Yahweh!* button to the right. The button name was a joke the user experience people had put in place until they could come up with something more scintillating, like *Submit* or *Ask*. (Debates were raging.) Sandra commandeered his chair, swiveled to the monitor, grabbed the keyboard, and began typing:

What the fuck is wrong with the universe—

"Sandra," George said, putting his hand over hers on the keyboard, "you might want to tone it down a bit. You know, we don't want to offend the server gods." His colleagues were fond of this expression.

She hit the backspace key and began again:

Given that good people who've done no wrong die every day—even young people like Johnny Savino Delano, one of the most considerate, sexiest, smartest men around—I would like to know the following: what is the likelihood that God exists?

She hovered the cursor over the *Ask Yahweh!* button.

"May I?" she said.

"That's exactly the sort of query that'll cause it to time out," he said, "but what the hell, might as well test the error messages. Go for it."

She clicked, the button appeared to depress, and a new browser window opened, displaying a progress bar and a message:

Processing query, please be patient!!

"That's my team's work," George said.

"Pretty," his daughter said, "and two exclamation marks, just to be sure." They watched as the progress bar filled with gold sparkles, then repeated the process a few times. After about a minute the response was displayed:

100%

George Warren looked at the screen, his expression frozen.

"I knew it!" Sandra said. "So God exists, and she's a bitch."

"Some of the engineers must be messing with us," George said. "I'm sure that's what this is. Try something else, but keep it simple. No extra verbiage."

She typed—

Does heaven exist?

And an immediate response pulsed onto the screen:

Sure does, girlfriend! And your daddy's going there real soon. Tell him to drive carefully.

"That's so stupid," Sandra said. "Okay, ha-ha on the whole thing. Your people are not even funny, like not at all. I'm sorry for wasting your time, Dad."

"Try again," he said, "something more. . . earthly, concrete." Now he was pissed off. Who'd gained access to the test code, and how long had it been going on?

He left his daughter at the computer, stepped out of his office, leaned out over the railing, and scanned the vast floor below for possible suspects. The ping pong game had ended and a young woman wearing big headphones and a military-style jumpsuit rocked back and forth as she typed up some code, which scrolled across her giant monitors. Nothing but dark empty offices rimmed the interior ring of the building. Then down below, out of the corner of his eye, he saw a green streak flash by—the undersole of a sneaker—and heard the whisper of corduroy directly below the catwalk. He ran down the steps.

It was Tagrin, an engineer who was hired a few months back, but whose presence had become a constant in the office since his first day. He was sitting himself down in his bean bag chair in his glass-walled office, holding his opened laptop in one big hand. Tagrin seemed never to go home, and George had on more than one occasion wanted to broach the topic of personal hygiene, especially when he was trapped with the giant man in a small conference room or was forced to stand next to him at a urinal.

George slid open his colleague's office door and stepped in.

"Was that you?"

"Was what me?"

"Are you playing around with the interface for Phase 3?"

"Phase 3—what are you talking about, George? We don't have anything up yet for Phase 3. Do we?"

"I have a few server clusters running the beta code."

"You're kidding. Hooked into the production back-end?"

"Yes," George said. He was suddenly a little cowed, realizing he was admitting a major breach of protocol. "For limited testing only," he added. To deploy binaries to the production back-end before running the code through a battery of QA test scripts—how insane could you be? It could mean his job.

"I see. Here on a Sunday and asking big questions, are we? Not about stocks—please tell me you're not asking for stock predictions. We haven't built the guardrails yet."

"It's for my daughter. A good friend of hers, her boyfriend actually, died recently, was killed. Anyway, long story short, I figured this would give her something to do. But now it looks like someone's playing a joke on us, a cruel joke. And they've gained access to my instance."

"I see." Tagrin looked up at a forty-five-degree angle toward George's office, as if his vision penetrated the intervening walls and ceiling. Then he moved his glance back to his computer, which rested on his generous lap, his legs splayed. His corduroy pants were worn bald on the inner thighs, the canvas uppers of his retro sneakers stained with drops of coffee—and probably urine, George thought.

"So, you weren't messing with the interface?" George said. "Because if you weren't, something odd is happening."

"Dad?" he heard his daughter shout. Both men looked up.

"Be right there." Then to Tagrin: "Well?"

"I haven't done a thing except make myself a doppio, see," and he pointed to a demitasse of coffee on his desk, "and now I'm updating my FB status. I have more friends than you can imagine. But. . . I have to ask, George, what do you think of our little engine-that-could, now that you've got your fingers firmly into it? Do you have any faith in the project at all?"

George wanted to remain neutral and politic, and was in no mood to begin a philosophical discussion of the grand existential—the metaphysical—endeavor. He'd already dug a deep enough hole for himself.

"I appreciate the project for sure."

"Appreciate it *for sure*? I see you, like I see everyone else from my little hovel down here. You wear that serious expression all the time, come in day in and day out without pause, almost never take time off. You had to when you found out about your daughter."

"It's called work, Tagrin. That's what you do—come in day in and day out. This is America."

"And you seem to despise me as much as everyone else."

"I'm not sure I understand what you mean." Though he did understand.

"You judge me purely by my physical characteristics, my outward-most mode of expression."

"That's human nature. And frankly, Tagrin, you could take better care of yourself, of your. . . outward-most mode of expression. Let me give you some advice—you need to shower more often, and wash your clothes once in a blue moon." He felt he was being cruel, too direct, but couldn't stop himself.

"Aha, the truth will out! Ten-thousand years ago you'd say to yourself, 'That's the big fellow from my tribe I smell at the back of the cave, and not an enemy. How nice. He must have returned from the hunt already. I feel safe, protected, loved.' But now there's no tolerance for such markers."

George had to admit this was true. "I guess not," he said. "At least not in the workplace."

"But I'll take it under advisement, your demand for cleanliness. Where I come from we don't find the need to scrub away our daily excretions."

"You raise a good point, Tagrin. Where do you come from, if I may ask?"

"You may ask."

A silence followed, with Tagrin re-engaged with his laptop.

"Look, about my being here, running the code in production—"

"Assuming you haven't crashed our data centers, your secret is safe with me. I won't tell anybody what you've done. And I don't buy that this is the first time you've done it, by the way."

"I appreciate that, I do," George said. "And sorry people are uptight about B.O. About those other queries, you have to understand—"

"Your wife is not cheating on you," Tagrin said. "You don't need a thousand server banks to figure that out. She's getting tired of your ways. You've got to keep things fresh. You know the drill. Haven't you tried porn yet?"

"You've been looking at the logs then?"

"Perhaps a tad. Now would you be so kind and hand me my espresso. By the way, what was your daughter's question?"

"Why God would take her boyfriend from her."

"I'm guessing God won't bring much solace. As far as I know, He's a fickle motherfucker," and Tagrin laughed with a generous heave of his gut and sank into his bean bag chair.

Sandra emerged onto the balcony above, resting her crutches on the railing and leaning over. "Dad, seriously, I tried again with something stupid-simple and now it's totally freaking out." She was looking down into Tagrin's office, her long nut-brown hair spilling forward over her shoulders and hiding her face in dark shadow.

When he arrived a half-minute later, his daughter and her crutches were gone and the monitor was cycling through bright and garish rainbow colors. He could hear its internal mechanisms clicking and hissing as if they were melting. Sandra couldn't have just scampered away, sight unseen. Confused, he called her name. When there was no response, he walked along the catwalk and looked into the empty offices along the way. No sign of her. He trotted down to the main floor and called into the women's bathroom, to no avail.

Scanning the rooms on the first floor—the micro-kitchen, rec room, the nook where the visiting massage therapist set up shop every Wednesday—he found no sign of his daughter, none at all.

"Have you seen her?" He leaned over and grasped the big engineer by the shoulders, shaking him so hard his head bobbled back and forth.

"Maybe now you understand what you've done," Tagrin said, composed as usual.

The woman engineer was peering over a cubicle wall, her bulbous headphones around her neck. She looked, George couldn't help thinking, like she belonged on the flight deck of an aircraft carrier.

"You remember Nabil?" Tagrin said.

"Yes. Took a transfer to the Paris office a few weeks ago, but what does that have to do with this?" He continued to scan the vast space for his daughter, his heart in turmoil.

"Well for your information, Paris thinks he's still working here."

"Really Tagrin, you've lost me. Get to the point."

"Like you, he launched Phase 3 code. Logs show that the sneaky bastard did it in the middle of the night about a month ago. Nobody else was here. I won't even tell you what the queries reveal. The point is, he hasn't been seen since. It's as if he vanished into the ether."

"Come on, Tagrin. Let's be adults here."

This was ridiculous and impossible, George thought. Yet a part of him believed Tagrin: the man's self-assured and knowing expression, even his great heft and odor somehow added legitimacy to his lunatic proclamation. . . that a man had simply vanished. How could he possibly explain any of this to Cheryl, that he'd lost their only child? And into the ether—what did that even mean? He was half deaf with the sound of blood pulsing past his tympanums. Then he smiled.

"You're joking, obviously."

"I wish I were," Tagrin said. "But there's no sense in panicking. I imagine our deity shows mercy now and then, mercurial as he is. God has his needs too; or hers; or its, if you prefer. Rumor has it he gravitates toward love, toward affection, tolerance and forgiveness. Nowadays you'll have to agree that real love and adoration, the spirit of cooperation and trust, these elements are all but gone from the human race, which I will tell you with one-hundred percent certainty, is bounding headlong toward a stupid, preventable annihilation, and the kernel of it all is that humanity's lost its humanity, as ironic—not to mention facile—as that sounds." He took one of George's hands in his giant, slightly sweaty paw. "Prove me wrong, George—prove that you have a chance at being truly human, and I can guarantee Sandra will be safe."

"Sorry?" said George, letting his hand be held.

"If you'd like your daughter back, you'll have to kiss me. Just a little peck gently on the lips. Kiss ol' stinky Tagrin for your daughter's return to the terrestrial realm."

"This is too much. You're out of your mind. She's got to be here." He pulled away and took off again.

"She's not," Tagrin said.

George ran at top clip around the first floor, checking every square foot of the place, ran up the steps and along the perimeter of each floor, even scoured the parking lot, which was mostly empty (the old Saab exactly where he remembered parking it, passenger seat still slid back all the way). Twenty minutes later, sweat streaming down his flushed face, he walked toward Tagrin, who was in the same exact spot, smiling.

"You've been standing here the whole time?" George said.

"It's what I do. And by the way, the previous offer stands."

George looked at the large, heart-shaped lips proffered him, not puckered or wanting of too much passion, but expectant and rimmed with dried coffee and razor stubble. He found himself putting one hand around the back of Tagrin's thick hairy neck, as if he knew no other way to kiss but to apply this love grasp, and then he moved in and before he knew it their lips were pressed together dryly, with Tagrin's steady breath now coming through his nostrils. It was not altogether unpleasant. Something about the kiss was reassuring, European. After a long moment the men separated.

"There there, you'll be fine," Tagrin said, holding one of George's hands again, then releasing it.

George's phone went off in his pocket. It was Cheryl.

"Where are you?" she asked. "You sort of vanished. Not the way to treat the women of your life, is it?"

He put his hand on Tagrin's shoulder to brace himself.

"The women of my life," George said.

"We're sitting here wondering what happened to you."

"I'm at the office. Sandra's with you?"

"Where else would she be? You're working? We thought you went out for. . . we weren't sure, to be honest. We were joking that you're coming back with a surprise for us. Sandra has her money on some Thai food from that new place on McLean Avenue. But you're at work—that's not the surprise we were hoping for."

"I'm coming home," he said, hanging up.

"Apparently she's with my wife in the apartment."

"Really?" Tagrin said. He turned, picked up his laptop with one hand and walked into his office, sitting himself down in the bean bag chair with a hiss.

Back at George's desk, the monitor had stopped its garish pulsing and was displaying an error:

Unsubstantiated strings. Query truncated. No results to return. You wanna try again?

From across the room Doris Amelia's granddaughter looked down on him in blurry multitudes.

He clicked the *Cancel* button.

As he pulled out of the parking lot, he noticed a little bit of Tagrin's stale coffee odor had stuck to him. Possibly it was on his neck, or on the collar of his weekend oxford.

On Route 9, heading south, he signaled left then crossed into the fast lane, accelerating until he was moving at a good clip. He looked right and saw at least a dozen sailboats plying the Hudson River. They were pitched low in a strong wind and seemed to be heading every which way, white triangles arranged in mirthful chaos.

He had the left lane all to himself, and he hit the gas harder still. Soon he would be home, soon he would see his women.

The Fate of Mathematicians

As he walked toward the lecture hall on the appointed evening, Max Tischler noticed that the campus heating plant, which was adjacent to and dwarfed by the auditorium, was venting steam in shapes resembling integers, shapes that broke apart and dissipated into the darkening September sky. The looming auditorium with its array of mirror-like windows and glass-fronted marble mezzanine was lit up and already strewn with bearded and be-bobbed mathematicians. Max had a quick thought, turned left, and walked to the campus pub, Mr. Bojangles, where he downed a pint of stout to steady himself.

The auditorium was packed with students, colleagues, visiting academics, hobbyists. Most of the students had stopped in at the university's cafeteria and now fed themselves from Styrofoam food boxes. The place smelled like vegetable shortening. A few of the PhD candidates had already delivered their talks, and now Professor Tischler would formally start the proceedings, welcome the visitors, get things going posthaste.

Max's chosen topic was pi, and he went on for some time about the advances made by the latest supercomputers, which had recently calculated the number to nearly ten trillion decimal places. He stood behind the lectern, keeping track of his notes with one hand while occasionally sweeping back his mop of black hair with the other. "And what a thrill," he said, "that we can now chain together a hundred thousand middling home computers for that high purpose, or devote an entire datacenter to exploring our beloved pi; and how breathless the world will be when quantum computing comes fully online—how humanity yearns to find the hidden patterns, to fill the known universe with the digits of pi. And yet. . . " he paused, letting his notes drop to the floor and spread around him, "and yet how ridiculous, how ludicrous we have become. You see my friends, that our tawdry base-ten system cannot rationally accommodate pi does not signify that pi is full of secrets."

Looking out onto the sea of half-bored faces with his practiced expression of omniscience, he noticed a woman with reddish hair and the broad, confident smile of a stage actress. She was sitting in the second row and wore a low-cut cerulean dress, a spot of color in a sea of ironic T-shirts.

"In our hubris," he went on, trying to ignore the woman, "we've come to believe that the number of fingers on our hands forms a more reasonable system of describing the universe than does the simple quotient of a circle's circumference," he paused, tracing that shape with his outstretched index finger, "divided by its diameter." He bisected it with a conductor's sweeping gesture. "This is an audacious assumption we've made. It reveals more about our egos as human beings than it does about the nature of pi. For as we all well know, pi is straightforward. A child has little difficulty understanding it."

He paused again, rubbed his eyes as if the whole exercise were excruciating.

"If I'm so unhappy about it, you might ask, why even talk about pi? Why welcome you all here with such strong opinions regarding this household number? Because, having surveyed the topics the esteemed guests are presenting at our university's fine colloquium on computational number theory, pi, in the guise in which I am currently discussing it, is among them, and an irrational number of times, if you will. Feel free to take offense at the following sentiment: it is as useful to calculate pi to its hundred-trillionth digit as it is to describe an automobile in terms of geese. It is an exercise in postmodern idiocy, a fashion statement that will go the way of bell-bottoms and acrylic ties." He bowed his head. "Thank you for coming, and enjoy your visit. Join me at the campus pub for further discussion." Applause—not exactly roaring—rose from the hall. Professor Tischler's analogies were generally considered dubious at first glance, persuasive after full consideration.

During the next few minutes the crowd cleared out and Max watched as the woman with the cerulean dress went with it. The overhead lights had recently been upgraded with a multitude of sensors, and now dimmed to near darkness, the presence of but a single man becoming immaterial. He turned the microphone off and collected his notes. Through one of the large skylights he watched a puffy 7 drift across the moonlit sky. Then he heard an auditorium door click shut. He turned to see the woman with the cerulean dress walking down the stepped aisle toward him. The lights came halfway on again. She'd apparently been having a cigarette outside, the last wisps of smoke drifting from her nostrils as she smiled.

"Do you follow the advances in the calculation of nitnerds?" was all he could think to say as she approached.

"I find the subject boring," she said.

"My feelings precisely," he said.

"It's good to see we still think alike, Max."

Well he had to admit that that smile of hers was certainly familiar.

"Do you mean to say you don't recognize me? Come on, you dope."

"There's definitely something there," he said. "Can't put my finger on it."

Yes, he knew her. No, he couldn't figure out from where.

"Maximilian, how could you forget me?"

"Don't be dramatic," he said. "You're not forgotten, but I don't know who you are, not exactly." It was all flooding back, if only she'd give him a few seconds.

"Wait," he said, "wait a moment." A small tornado of memory snapshots, like faded photographs, was spinning around the inside of his skull, running up against the soft rubber of his brain. And all at once he knew who she was, could not have missed it now that he saw that smile, that figure of hers.

"Rhonda Bryce," he finally said, "DeCanyon College, class of '88."

"Bra-vo," she said, "only now it's Rhonda Millner." R. Millner— he'd seen that name on the roster of guest speakers for the colloquium. She was scheduled to go on tomorrow.

"It's been such a long time," he said. "I'd nearly forgotten about you. . . " No, that wasn't right, he'd certainly not forgotten. "What I mean is it's been so long that I'd lost hope of seeing you again." Too dramatic. "I mean to say—"

"It's all okay," she said, clearing the air with the gentle swipe of her hands.

"Yes, that's it—thank you. It's all okay. And you're married now."

"His name was Elroy and I loved him dearly, and he dropped dead of a burst aorta two years ago. Least I could do was keep the name."

Way back then at DeCanyon College, she and Max, both math majors, had been in the same Fortran class and soon began meeting at the computer lab in the evenings. They'd code late into the night, helping each other with their homework assignments, basking in the isolation of the computer lab while keeping each other company. Those nights had made Max unhappy and giddy at the same time, depressed and euphoric, the side effects of staring at those phosphorescing mainframe consoles for long stints, of creating nested do-loops until he couldn't keep his eyes open. But at least he'd had his constant companion, Rhonda, typing and mumbling at his side.

They started collaborating on their Fortran routines, and he was happy, thrilled to know that their code was intertwined, an intimacy few others would have understood. Soon they were having late-night sessions in Max's dorm room to work through other assignments. They'd puzzle out linear algebra transformations or join their minds to write witty proofs of theorems already proved.

The recollection of one of these sessions had always haunted Max, a memory he now tried to hold at bay. Despite his efforts over the years, recalling the scene tended to elicit a stabbing pain in his intestines, as if he'd swallowed a fork all those years ago. Rhonda must be waiting for him to say something intelligible. Yet he could only think about how much, despite what time had done to them both, she still resembled the young woman he'd known way back then. The undergrad, that is, who showed up at his dorm room one night in April soaked through for having been caught in a deluge. His roommate was across the hall getting stoned with some Deadheads. The college radio station was playing The Cure, something sullen and apt, which was crackling out of his boombox. He had never seen her body so clearly outlined, her breasts and crescent-shaped buttocks lurking under the gripping cotton. She was shivering, and he was genuinely concerned for her health. "I washed these," he'd said, offering her a neatly folded stack of his clothing. "Put your stuff in the dryer downstairs and put these on or you'll catch a cold. But. . . I mean. . . not in that order. First put these on, then put your stuff in the dryer."

She'd looked at the stack of clothing. It seemed neither of them could imagine her actually wearing any of it.

"Would it bother you much if I don't?"

She did accept his offer of a towel and dried her hair and patted down her clothing. Before long they were flipping through their assignments, wondering aloud whether they could get away with working on a single extra credit program, each handing in a tweaked version of the other's. Would the teaching assistant even notice?

She was sitting on his velveteen lounger and he was on the floor facing her, his legs crossed. Rhonda leaned back and her skirt rode up her thighs in a way that seemed impossible to ignore. Yet she, at least, ignored it—or that was the impression she wanted to give—or he felt she wanted to give. He could see her pallid inner thighs beneath that denim skirt, he could see the whiteness of her underwear, the slight shadow of her pubic hair bristling beneath. She was holding the lab handout in front of her face and he imagined her smiling behind it. Then he leaned forward, his pulse slow but forceful, and placed his hand on her knee, index finger pointing up her skirt. Oh God, how he had wanted to be with her. Rhonda, keeping her face behind the book, moved her thigh backward a few inches, leaving Max's hand dangling in midair, still pointing to the place he had been thinking about ever since.

Instead of being persistent in the way of most young men, he never made another advance toward her, feeling it would be untoward and disrespectful. At least their academic partnership was a success in the end. They both received high grades in Fortran, linear algebra, and another class or two, long ago faded from memory. Their code was probably still intermingled on a roll of magnetic tape in some far-off storage site of the university or, more likely, under a thousand feet of garbage in a landfill. Losing its charge by the day.

After DeCanyon, Max shunted himself to graduate school in New England and it wasn't long before he was overtaken by the thrill of academia, only occasionally allowing his thoughts to journey back to his years at DeCanyon. Finally he found companionship and affection and sex from a grad school classmate named Narice, who found him to be intellectually rigorous, which, oddly, she equated with virility. She had turned down a kiss the first date, but he persisted in the courtship, and by the fourth date they'd slept together. Narice was interested in one topic only: astronomy. She came of age in rural New York, Delaware County, where she claimed that "on clear nights the blanket of stars lights up the trees even when the moon is new." This always sounded somehow backwards to him, but she always said it when she was drunk and wistful, and he never grew tired of hearing it. She'd told him how her adolescence amounted to countless hours of tedious schoolwork and humiliation shoveled on her by classmates. Undergrad life was no better. The exception was calculus, which thrilled her as soon as she understood it; with no effort at all she could sketch conical hyperboloids, or the surfaces of ellipsoids as if lit poignantly by a setting sun. It was all of a piece, the light of her childhood illuminating everything she thought and did.

That Narice and Max had found each other was a miracle, and enough to keep them ecstatic for the first year of their relationship. During the second year their having found one another still seemed a happy circumstance. By then he was deep in the throes of number theory and combinatorics. Narice was offered a job at the Jet Propulsion Laboratory in California, and off she went, leaving Max to his numeration of the innumerable, the light gone out of it, mostly.

After that he'd had a few flings here and there, but nothing approaching what he'd had with Narice, who would sometimes nibble the edges of his shoulders as she came down from her orgasms. She would talk of seeing his face, the way he looked when he was on top of her, even after she closed her eyes.

"It's not a bad thing," she'd say, "that face of yours, all that happy effort."

After he landed his present professorship, Max settled into an ascetic but not unhappy version of the academic life. He often said to himself that if loneliness were necessary to excel in his field, then he would embrace it much as he would a lover. He reminded himself that plumbing the abstract depths of human perception was not an easy job. But he had no regrets. During those late nights working his pad and pencil until the sun popped over the brick buildings across the street, it seemed to him that he was probing not some unseen property of the universe, but that he was working to decipher loneliness itself, as if the emotion sprung from a theorem, or was a force similar to gravity.

And now, without warning, Rhonda had stepped into this purposeful vacuum, stepped into it with her ridiculously out of place dress, her beaming smile, her hair shimmering, her lips full of color. He hoped she was through mourning her Elroy Millner, though he certainly didn't want to get ahead of himself. He looked into her eyes as deeply as nonchalance would permit. Something had changed, physically changed. What he remembered as uneventful light brown eyes were now flecked with spots of black. That's what happens when death reaches into your heart, he thought.

One reason he hadn't immediately recognized her was because her hair had been short at DeCanyon, in a kind of nondescript, careless tousle, with straight bangs framing her face.

Now she told him she'd been doing research for a genetics lab in Louisiana where she had developed a unique index for representing the degree of "psychic disbalance" of an individual's genome. This was her specialty—computational genomics and its implications for psychiatry.

"They say I'm helping to decipher God's handiwork. But I want to teach, Max, like you," she said. "I'm tired of the private sector, of the company smock. The flunkies in their suits asking for status reports, impactful metrics—I'm sick of all of it. I want my flock of sheep too.

"I'll be damned, Max Tischler," she added, stepping to the edge of his shoes and surveying his face, "it's been too long. The least you can do is buy me a drink, a soft one."

"Come over for dinner instead," he said. He knew he was being reckless now. "I'll cook. We'll hang out like old times. We don't even have to talk about math." She nodded slowly, either to show she accepted the invitation, or that she merely understood it. "I need to make a stop at the pub first and take my beating."

"But they love you here, don't they?"

In his apartment, over the remains of a rotisserie chicken, a pot plastered with Minute Rice, and an empty liter of RC Cola, they talked about probability, the fallacy of chaos, and the pets they'd loved and lost over the years. He recommended that next time she came to visit she wear something warmer than the airy number she'd had on at his lecture. Nights get cold, he said. But it was a moot sentiment, since at that moment she was wearing jeans. . . like she used to.

She lifted one foot onto the chair and nuzzled it under the opposite thigh. She began flicking her hair, ringlets and all, from one side to the other, then a few moments later, back again.

"I'm definitely warm now," she said, lighting a cigarette. She watched Max's eyes drift down her body, then back up to her face. "Why is it that you never tried to kiss me?" she said. "We spent so much time with each other and all we did was talk and study." The soda had kicked in, he could see, the caffeine making her eyes a bit wild, her voice edgy. "Such a shy boy. I wanted you to ask me out. It was always convergent series with you, or limit points, the babble of an undernourished genius. It's not as though you're a bad looking man, you know."

"I was a fool," he said. Lifting himself from his chair, he leaned over and kissed her on the lips, lightly. She turned for more. He took her hand and guided her to the living room, to a love seat.

They began kissing again but a blast of sound from outside broke their concentration. The garbage truck, a commercial number, was collecting the trash from the Italian restaurant across the street. This was not unexpected. Max could have predicted that they'd come around this night at this time, as always. What he could not have predicted was the lunacy, that something had gone wrong with the mechanics of the great machine: the sound echoed off the brick facades of the buildings along his narrow block with such a piercing ferocity—as if the roaring diesel engine itself were sitting in his living room—that Rhonda pushed him off in mid-kiss, their lips having met for only a few seconds.

"Wow," she said, "that's something."

"Damn garbage guys," Max said. "I'll murder them. The whole bunch."

Then cars started bleating their horns. This was also typical, how things progressed when the haulers passed through. These drivers who were unfortunate enough to be behind the garbage truck were now trapped, so they honked their horns. It seemed to Max that they contemplated their existences with horn honks. Horn honks would allow them to transcend their incommodious lives.

"Honk honk," he said to Rhonda. "Honk honk. People are ludicrous."

They had squeezed themselves onto the loveseat, their legs intertwined. He went to kiss her again, but she moved away.

"Sorry," she said, "but how do you deal with that racket?"

"Simple. I put it out of my mind."

And soon they were kissing yet again, deeply, and he was moving his hands toward her breasts. But as his mind raced ahead to the moment of contact, he realized that he could not hold a vision. The noise of the garbage rig had now realized a pleading, keening pitch that was capable of piercing the primeval human heart. In its existential terror, it conjured the image of lonely men and women hunched over and weeping like lost children in dark houses, mud huts and prison cells around the world, which was but a giant den of misery.

Then Rhonda broke away from him, stood up.

"There's no way that kind of noise is legal." Her eyes were moist, tears on the verge of cresting. Max saw his redemptive night slipping away. His windows were shut tight and locked, and still the sound permeated the air. She parted his faded velvet curtains and looked out at the garbage truck. "Not in such a quiet residential neighborhood—how can it be *allowed?* Can't the cops write a summons for something like that?" The sound increased and Max's Corning ware set, deep inside his kitchen cupboard, began rattling. Rhonda's pupils had grown large and now only the slightest ring of her speckled irises encircled them.

He opened the window and looked down on the street. It was raining. A street lamp flickered, seeming to suspend the drops in midair a thousand at a time. Six stories below he could see the long berm of garbage bags stacked on the curb three high and three deep, and the garbage men were in no rush. They never were. They threw a few bags into the hopper, talked, laughed—it looked like laughter, the way they shook—and then one of them would cycle the blades while the other one surveyed the line of trapped cars receding into the night. Max could hear distant horn honks, timorous and losing hope.

"I'll go down and talk to those men."

"You wouldn't. Would you?" A little smile, somewhat devious, cut across Rhonda's face. He got a good look at her teeth which, like the greatest of Athenian temples, had once seen better days.

The first thing Max noticed as he stepped from his building's stoop was the familiar stench of trash. The air itself seemed to be viscous. The garbage bags were stacked in front of the restaurant directly across the street, beads of rain glimmering on their green plastic skin.

"A lot of bags out here tonight," he shouted to the closer of the two haulers during a brief pause in the hydraulics. The man gave a start and spun around. He raised his spattered safety goggles.

"What's that?" he said. He was a white man and had the face of a kid, a large round visage with a small, pouty mouth and bloodshot eyes that seemed shrunken from fatigue, from overwork.

"I said, lots of bags."

"Too many," the hauler shouted back. "These guys always got too many. Where in hell do they come from is what I wanna know." Then he lowered his goggles and began throwing his charges into the hopper, one after another. His partner, who was hidden on the opposite side of the truck, cranked down a handle, cycling the blades.

One of the bags split under the pressure, spilling out fist-sized pieces of a fleshy, sponge-like material. When the bag split open completely a few football-sized eggplants rolled out. "Aubergine is what they call 'em in the restaurant business," the hauler shouted, apparently seeing the puzzled look on Max's face. He tossed another bag into the hopper, which was filled with a viscous brown mash. "That's all these bags ever have in them—aubergine, aubergine, aubergine."

Looking up at his apartment, Max saw Rhonda standing between the parted black curtains. Due to a combination of the vertiginous angle and the narrow strip of light in which she stood, she seemed thick-set, almost monstrous behind that window. And she was watching him. "What I'd like to know," the hauler continued, "is where the hell they're all comin' from. They must be growing 'em in the basement or something."

Max felt a clicking beneath his sternum, a signal that his mitral valve was emphatically prolapsing, or so he imagined. "It's a good question," he said to the hauler, "the mystery of the replicating aubergines." The hauler looked a bit mystified by that. "But I'm wondering," Max went on, "if you guys could come back to finish this up some other time. Much later tonight, or tomorrow."

The hauler with the child's face and the small, overburdened eyes froze, holding a bag over the hopper. Now suddenly he seemed able to hear every word Max said.

"What are you, some kind of a joker? When's most convenient for you? Hey Charlie," he shouted to his partner, "let's get outta here and come back when the prof here says it's okay."

Charlie, still hidden, laughed. "Indeed, sire, let us!"

"I'm thinking that there must be a better time, is all."

"This is our shift. What options you think we have?"

Max reached for his wallet. "I understand you're doing your job. I'll give you a little something and you come back in two hours. Here, take the money."

The hauler raised his goggles for a second time. His head sat on a thick, short neck, which, in turn, widened into broad uneven shoulders. "What do you think we are, idiots, automatons? Not yet, buddy, not yet. Soon enough, but not yet. We've got families." Suddenly Max was off the ground. Charlie had come up behind him and now had him in a half nelson. Both men were laughing as they threw Max into the hopper. He struggled to get out, but the perfectly smooth steel, covered in slippery liquid, was impossible to grasp. The men pretended to fight each other for the lever that controlled the hydraulics. Who would get to crush Max to death? This game had them doubling over in fits.

As he struggled, he could hear an increase in both frequency and severity of horn honks, as if drivers were either enjoying the entertainment or concerned for his wellbeing. In either case, nobody got out of his car.

Every time Max summoned the strength to stand upright in order to climb out, he was tapped lightly by Charlie, and fell back onto the hopper. Charlie was tall and wiry, an extruded, darker, possibly Trinidadian version of the other hauler. (They both wore matching goggles along with beige coveralls emblazoned with their employer's logo.) He laughed freely, like a child playing in a sprinkler. Max came to understand that at any moment he would be crushed in the gaping maw of this truck and reduced to nothing more than trash in a city that had plenty of it.

Finally, he managed to grab hold of the outer lip of the hopper and hoist himself to, tumbling onto the asphalt of East Morton Street. He hobbled backward toward the foyer of his building all the while watching the men, their eyes ablaze with pure joy, a happiness unburdened and full of delight. He was their catharsis for the week. The action of digging for his keys in his garbage-packed pockets caused the haulers to lean on each other for support, so faint were they. Stage left, cars were honking in continuous blasts and flashing their high-beams. An ancient sub-compact in the form of a Honda Civic leapt up onto the sidewalk and sped past the truck, passing six inches in front of Max.

When he opened the door to the apartment, Rhonda was curled up on the love seat, her downcast face hidden in the grandeur of her tousled hair.

"This is an awful city, isn't it?" she said.

"So you saw?"

"Some of it."

"Why didn't you come down? Why didn't you help me? At least you could have called the cops."

"Really, is that what you wanted, help? I don't believe it. I haven't seen you for ages, Max, but one thing I can still say for sure: you could use this sort of thing. Someone needed to break that hard shell of yours."

"You're kidding. Break my shell?"

"You don't see the need?"

"No, I don't. Not exactly," he said. "Excuse me, but I have to jump in the shower. I'm sure you understand."

His clothes made a splashing sound when he dropped them onto the tile floor.

A few minutes later he alighted from a cloud of steam, a towel wrapped around his waist. "You know," he said, suddenly becoming aware of Rhonda's eyes on his body, "it was the noise that pushed me over the edge. The noise, and seeing how much it upset you. But I can't say I'm happy that you saw all that, and did nothing, nothing at all. Additionally—"

"No more talk," she said. She led him into the bedroom. Standing in the trapezoid of streetlight coming in through the curtains, she began to undress. Max, wrapped in his white towel and rising to the occasion cartoonishly, waited for the full reveal. He'd already spent a generation imagining what he'd missed. Now she stood before him fully bared, his beautiful regret. Her bush was neatly trimmed into an equilateral triangle, something out of a Picasso, he thought. They both smiled at it, and he supposed the joke might have been shared by like-minded geometers around the world. "And what about you, dear friend?" she said, leaning forward and releasing his towel, which briefly snagged before dropping to the floor.

Next day, as Max walked across the quad, the sun seemed to have a benevolence that permeated his every cell. He was on his way back from the university's infirmary, where they'd put a metal splint on one of his fingers. Sprained during his fight with the hopper, it had turned blue from the second joint up. In his mind he was drafting a letter to the hauling company describing the incident objectively. He decided not to seek legal action or even to suggest that the haulers be terminated. Rhonda was right after all—he owed something to those two men. They were a terrible duo, but they'd performed a sort of miracle of chiropractic, unsprang his coiled soul, beating him into happiness. And now. . . now all that he saw before him was heightened and distorted. He couldn't be sure how long the spell would last, but at the moment objects seemed surrounded by a pulsing corona of bluish-gray haze. An old Chevy Impala parked by the chemistry lab. . . its fenders seemed inlaid with swirling polka-dots. As he walked beneath a row of poplars, a gust of wind swept through the leaves. They flashed like silver dollars and rustled like a million tiny bells. He nearly cried at the strange beauty of it all.

Dr. Rhonda Millner stood behind the lectern describing her invention of blade equations, an algorithmic sieve that she deployed to "slice our genomic code into mathematically digestible snippets." Max, unshaven, with a few bruises visible on his face, was in the third row, watching her hands as she withdrew a piece of string from her breast pocket, her amplified voice carrying across the packed auditorium. "We all know that the biological subtleties that individuate each of us are coded into our genetic material." She deftly looped the string into a flattened corkscrew on the overhead projector. "But some say even our personalities, our petty likes and dislikes, our broad inclinations—a bent toward cruelty or kindness, for example—they all reside within this giant molecule. And I tend to agree. Western culture has always used the heart as the metaphor for the soul, for the root of moral character and our capacity for love." Catching sight of Max, she stepped out from the projector's glare and squinted to look at him, to take in his face. The auditorium was quiet and several chairs squeaked as attendees turned to locate the object of her gaze. And there was Max, smiling back at her dreamily as if he were being serenaded. Regaining her composure, she placed a color transparency depicting a coiled DNA molecule on the glass.

"But while the heart analogy is hard-coded into our cultural psyches, I believe we'll come to see the double-helix as a better metaphor—for our hearts, if you will. Because it *is* humanity's symbol, a cipher encoded with three-and-a-half billion years of bad habits. And that's where I come in, to help figure out the whole mess."

As he watched her, Max felt a palsied tap on his shoulder and knew it was Dr. Dellahoussaye, the dean of the math department. Dellahoussaye was nearing ninety, and approaching retirement asymptotically. "She's something, isn't she?" he said. "Are you aware that we've been negotiating with her for the last three months? It looks like she's on board at last. I think she'll make a fine addition. I understand you two were classmates down at DeCanyon."

"We used to study together," Max said, taking a very deep breath. "She's the brightest of the bright."

Prague's Children

When he considered the alternatives, he wasn't so bad off. For one, he was still breathing. Dying in his sleep was an ongoing fear of Gregor's, and every morning that he awoke with dull sunlight pushing into his room brought relief. In that manner, at least, these first few moments of consciousness conjured the usual cheerful reaction—he was still alive!

But it's true that the rest was worrisome, more as each second passed and the realization of his transformed body sank in. His parents and sister had only recently accepted that, despite all their doubts about him, he would manage to make his way in this world. They understood that Gregor's talents and skills allowed him not only to carry on as a competent individual, but to support them as well—to put food on the table and pay the rent.

Now he would have to deal with this unexpected inconvenience.

He slid out of bed and hit the ground with a thud, then heard movement on the other side of his bedroom door. It must be his sister, or his mother. And the sun was already coming through his windows at an angle that told him he'd overslept. This was almost as offensive to him as his transformation.

What was he to do? Leave, leave now, until the spell passed.

He recalled that his fellow traveling salesman, Thomas, a thoughtful young bachelor of limited means, lived down the block. He had complained to Gregor numerous times about the confinement of his flat, how it was in the basement, the only window in the place peeking at the street as if a voyeur. All day long he had the view of trousers and dresses, work shoes—walking canes and umbrellas constantly clanged against the window grate. Thomas's flat was a stone's throw from Charlotte Street, where Gregor and his family lived. If indeed his condition was not imagined, if it proved robust ("impossible," "impossible," he kept repeating to himself quietly), he would have to make the short journey. He imagined his friend opening that street-level window for Gregor, who could crawl right in. There he would find sympathy and protection.

As morning gave way to day, his condition was unchanged. Through his bedroom door he begged to be left alone, claiming, in his squeaky new voice, to have an issue with his throat, refusing offers of tea or warm milk, and insisting that he not be disturbed so that he might rest and heal.

Sometime after midnight, after the narrow streets finally went quiet, Gregor checked on himself again, conferring with his little legs that he could now waver them in the air one at a time, and confirming the clarity of his multiplied vision which was, nonetheless, unified.

He opened his bedroom window and found it easy to grasp the exterior wall with his claws as he climbed down. Once on the cobblestones he moved like lightning to the small window of Thomas's flat.

Reaching through the metal grate, Gregor tapped on the window, tapped again, until a light came on. Long horizontal shadows moved along the walls below. And then a sight that brought terror and relief at once: a pair of antennae moved beneath the window. This was followed by scampering sounds, a crash as books and a lamp fell to the floor, and finally by a high-pitched yelp. Gregor tapped again on the window, this time with panic. The street seemed quiet and abandoned, true, and none of the windows around him were lit, but he was worried that before long somebody would come strolling down the narrow street, or that Thomas's racket would stir the interest of his neighbors.

In another moment, the noise stopped and Thomas's face rose to the window.

"It's me, Gregor," Gregor said in his new voice.

The face was terrified on the other side of the glass—the face, that is, of a large insect, with its beclouded and multifaceted eyes that darted back and forth, one then the other.

"Let me in," Gregor said, "so that we can discuss our situation."

Thomas fumbled for a time before unlocking the window, and then the metal grate. Gregor slid in through the opening, landing on the fainting couch below the window.

"What has happened?" Thomas said. "This is a dream. A nightmare."

"If so, I have not awakened for a full day and night," Gregor said.

Thomas looked at himself in a small mirror that had fallen to the ground. Then he looked at Gregor, then at his reflection again. "What legs we have," he said. "How are we to go about in town? And work, by God, it will be impossible to hold a pencil to paper."

"Calm down," Gregor said, and then paused until Thomas stopped flicking his little limbs about. "And thank you for letting me in. I remembered your talk of the little window."

"I've said many times that you are always welcome to drop in, as are all my friends. Though naturally I never expected the invitation to be literal. Whatever shall we do with ourselves?"

Just then the window's metal grate squeaked as it was lifted. Another of them, this one with a dustier color and more of a burnish to its carapace, slid through the opening, landed on the small couch, bounced off it, and nearly hit Gregor as it came to a halt.

"You, you there, I saw you scamper into this place," said the creature to Gregor in its young and familiar-sounding voice. He surmised that it was one of the apprentices who had found his way to them. "I have been climbing the walls and gutter spouts all night! Is this the thanks one gets for joining your fine firm? This is intolerable. I am engaged to be married. I can't receive a dowry in such a condition." Gregor was about to reassure the young man (as it were) that they were all in this together, and Thomas was still engaged in self-examination, when the grate sprung open again, and yet another of them somersaulted in, and then, shortly after that, another, until, it seemed, word had spread throughout town that Thomas' small flat was the safe haven for these newly transformed citizens.

In the morning a bolt of sunlight came in through the window, removing any doubt that this might be but a nightmare.

Because his fellow salesmen were on the road so often, it was rare to have them all in one place at the same time. Mixed in with the terror and disorientation, an unusual feeling of camaraderie took hold. Even the managing clerk, Karl, who always kept tabs on their commissions and was generally disliked, nodded to Gregor's proclamation that calm and forethought were the way forward. He stopped his quivering and sat as best he could upon the fainting couch which was, Gregor realized, a piece of furniture well suited to their new physiques. Karl had among them embodied the most profound drop in stature, from managing the men to being merely one of the more terrified insects among them. Pitying him, nobody questioned his usurpation of the most comfortable seat in the flat.

Sasha, a young woman who often stopped by the office to sell pastries to the men who were about to go on the road, was also among them, though nobody knew this until she suddenly shouted, in what was clearly a tremulous and feminine voice, "What am I to do?" from the other end of the room. Her antennae were crossing each other like swords. "I am full of eggs—my belly is swollen with eggs!" (None of them had yet mastered the anatomical terms for their new bodies.) Indeed, the sticky spheres were already being discharged and were densely strewn about her corner of the room. A scent like lavender rose from them. The others moved out of the way and gave her what little space they could. She seemed embarrassed, but unable to stop laying them.

"Who has done this?" Gregor said. All were silent, but soon a meek voice could be heard.

"It was I," it said. This was Edgar, a clerk who had been a quiet and small man, even among all the other quiet and small men of the firm, though as an insect he seemed somehow thicker and better armored than the rest. "She. . . " he said, then he looked at Sasha. . . "You had flicked a wing up as we made our way here, and I couldn't help myself. You felt *something*, didn't you? But I do certainly apologize for the violation."

"Look what you've done," Sasha said, acknowledging her appeal, but wanting nothing to do with it. "More of us littering the streets before long, that's all we need. Am I to wait around and care for my nymphs?" This was more than any of them had anticipated. She moved heavily to a large armoire in the corner, opened the door, and pressed her hind quarters into it so that they could not be accessed, nor her egg-laying seen. Edgar moved away from her and wore a guilty expression, as far as these things could be ascertained.

"Nothing should surprise us," Gregor said. "Does this account for everyone in the office?" There was a grumbling as each of the large insects assessed the crowd. Many of them counted all the individuals present. "Less those on the road, the count is correct," said Karl. "I can't precisely say who is who, but we all seem to be present in aggregate. The Director is not here, but he is rarely in the office and as you know his own staff occupies the floor above ours. Perhaps they, too, have been stricken. Or perhaps they have been spared."

"That's not our concern," Gregor said. He had always wanted to punch the Director anyway.

They stayed in the small flat for nearly two days, frittering away the time, eating everything in Thomas's kitchen, which is to say not much at all. They were disconcerted to learn that the aged orange peels and cheese rinds that had been sitting in the garbage were to all of them as tasty as honey and chocolate, pleasures to be divided up and savored.

On the afternoon of the second day, a loud rapping against the door silenced the room. Then they heard the human voice of the Director on the other side of the door.

"Now then," he said to someone, probably an assistant clerk, "who have we here again?"

"Thomas, a junior salesman, sir."

"We've really worked our way down. Try again," and the rapping ensued, only more fiercely.

"Is anybody home?" the second voice said.

A minute passed, the inhabitants of the apartment frozen in fear and anticipation.

"How unorthodox," the Director finally said. "We'll have to start hiring replacements immediately. Shouldn't be difficult. Come, let us give up this hopeless search. People have no work ethic, none at all these days," and they listened to his cane ticking down the hallway until all went silent again.

"We need to get out of this place!" someone said. "We're bound to be discovered. And the air in here is terrible."

"Agreed," mumbled two or three others.

"To be completely honest," Thomas said, "my hospitality has run out, as has my food."

Gregor remembered that his uncle Stanko, a farmer who was known for his extraordinary mushrooms, came in from the countryside every Wednesday to sell his goods at one of the markets. He was one of Gregor's favorite relatives, always giving him big hugs and presenting to his mother (Stanko's sister) a bundle of marinated and dried mushrooms that would last the family through the winter.

"I have an idea," Gregor said.

Stanko had always set up his mushroom stand in Losos Square, where he had a reserved spot at the edge of one of the arcades of shops, in one of the small dorsal indentations that provided a semi-private setting.

So on the third evening of his transformation, Gregor found himself setting forth on his own, navigating the rooftops and lesser-known alleyways of the city, scurrying under cover of shadows, seeking out uninhabited swaths of muddy passageways, skirting drunks and opium addicts (to them he was safely a figment), and on occasion finding a tasty morsel. He arrived on the outskirts of Losos Square as the vendors were packing up their equipment, loading them into satchels and carts, hitching them to beasts of burden. Gregor stayed in the shadows of a narrow alleyway, at the end of which he could see his uncle sitting on his stool, grown grayer and more grizzled than he remembered. He moved down the little alleyway, finding shelter behind a pile of splintered wood not five yards from his uncle, who anyway seemed as jolly as ever, mumbling to himself as he packed up his empty baskets and shook out canvas tablecloths.

"Uncle," Gregor said. "It's me, Gregor," but the old man paid no attention, or did not hear. He tried again, "Uncle Stanko, sir, it is your nephew, Gregor." The old man stopped folding a tablecloth and turned around, glancing down the alleyway. He must have caught sight of one of Gregor's antennae, which he was unable to tuck out of view.

"Hello?" Stanko said.

"Yes, hello," Gregor said. "It is Gregor. Your sister's son."

"Yes, Gregor? It does not sound like you, and why are you hiding?"

"I must warn you, Uncle. I have changed since you've last seen me. Changed quite a lot. But I have come here specifically to find you. Please stay where you are and make no sound as I reveal myself."

"Aren't you a bit old to be playing these games?"

"Do you promise?" Gregor said. "I'm going to reveal myself now. Restrain yourself. Do not cry out." He scampered fully into view, though remained in a long shadow. "I'm harmless, Uncle. I do not bite."

Stanko held the tablecloth in mid-fold, squinting into the darkness of the alleyway. At first he looked in the wrong place, as if a man would emerge from the shadows, but when he turned his glance downward, there stood Gregor.

At first leaping back, Stanko then fixed himself to the ground, staring down at the creature and catching his breath. "Oh, my poor poor boy. How long have you been ill?"

"Three days. I believe that's right. Yes, three days now. I can't go to work; I fear for my life being around. . . people. You must not say a word to my family. They would die of shame if they were to see me like this."

"Don't worry," he said. "It's a small wonder that has befallen you. But why have you come to me?"

Most people would have been reduced to a shivering mass of human frailty, but here stood his uncle, calm and composed, broad of shoulder. He even finished folding the tablecloth.

"You. . . live far from here. In the countryside. I thought that perhaps. . . "

"I see. Provide you with shelter?"

"Yes, Uncle. You've always been kind. You and Helen have always shown yourself to be generous souls. Is she still sick? I know this is the oddest request you've ever had, and I wouldn't ask unless it was the only solution I could imagine."

Stanko considered the situation in silence, all the while turning to look this way and that, rubbing his scruff, rolling and unrolling his shirt sleeves. He seemed to be calculating odds of some kind.

Then a smile cut across his face. "You can stay with us. We are family, after all."

"Thank you, Uncle. But I'm afraid it's not simple. There are more of us."

"How many more?"

"We are ten in all."

"Ten. Well now that's something else entirely. Do you know them? Are they well behaved?"

"They're my colleagues. We are all peaceful and need only escape the city until we can find a cure, or. . . Oh, it's too much to think about. I assume we cannot all go with you. That's understandable. I will send as many as you can take, and I will remain here. Let me say that we would be quiet, that we would help where we could. In addition, you will find that we would not compete with food for you, for it seems we prefer to eat, how shall I say it—scraps."

"And what else?" Stanko said. "You will not mate with one another; you will not destroy my property."

"I promise."

"Let me think, let me think. Ten of you, you say."

Gregor hid himself behind the pile of wood scraps as his uncle mulled it over, continuing to pack up his goods. Finally, he approached the pile and spoke directly to Gregor.

"Where should I pick everyone up?"

Gregor gave him the address of Thomas's flat.

"When I am done here, I will bring my cart. Please get everyone ready."

It was strange to have a man standing among them in the small flat. They had all become used to their new perspective from so close to the ground. Stanko towered above them all, though was perhaps half again their volume on average.

"I'll take two of the larger ones at a time, or three of the medium-sized ones. You'll fit comfortably in my cart. I'll cover you with my tarpaulin. Ah, there's still some daylight left. Let's wait a few moments longer. We'll have all of you to my place by sunrise."

And so they were all carted north to his uncle's land, a sprawling and quiet Bohemian estate of dense woodlands and a few ponds here and there on which the insects were told they were free to roam at will.

For weeks they wandered unfettered, digging burrows, testing their new bodies, trying to bear the absolute and impenetrable reality of their condition. One evening in the dying heat of late July, Stanko sent word that he'd like them all to meet at the main barn, a structure from which, hoisted high upon a hay loft, he often assayed his estate through a great looking glass.

Stanko stood beside Karl at the front of the hall, the latter looking embarrassed, with mud spattered on his underside, his antennae droopy, a few deep scratches along his carapace.

"Now then, it's wonderful to see all of my new friends in one spot. I think you all know Karl."

The hall filled with a quiet chattering—yes yes, we know him.

Gregor noticed that a few of the insects had blades of grass stuck in their joints and small twigs and gravel protruding from the seams of their exoskeletons. This seemed to be a small price to pay for their continued existence, for life had at last become tolerable once again. On some days Gregor even managed to enjoy himself, roaming freely around the woods, eating grubs and bark and dung, chattering with his former colleagues in their newfound tongue.

"I have found it good and well to host my nephew and his outcast friends, and you are and will always be free to roam at your leisure, to find shelter beneath the roof of this barn and any others when the weather turns. You seem to have no predators, for what creature would dare attack the likes of you!" And here he laughed, but those in attendance were silent, even nervous. What was the old graybeard leading up to, gathering them all here, regaling them with sentiments of his own goodness? "There remains one small question," he said, "that of how you might compensate my wife and me for our hospitality. You see we have no children of our own, nobody who might support us in our advancing age. We struggle even to pay our taxes, and my wife's hands are swollen with arthritis after years of work. Ask your Gregor. He will tell you that she's never seen in town because she is so ill. We do not run a hotel, no matter our instincts for kindness and generosity. Which brings us back to our friend, Karl. We have been conducting some research, you see, and wouldn't you know it, but your kind is significantly better at finding mushrooms than I or my farmhands." With his big knuckles he rapped Karl on his elytra. The sound was like knocking on a hardwood door. "I would surmise that you are the best mushroom hunters our noble Bohemia has ever known."

Karl hung his head low.

"You see my friends, you have untold talent in the field of mycology. You can smell the little delicacies from hundreds of meters away—you seem able to smell them even through the soil, leaves, and manure. And with those limbs—all those wonderful limbs of yours—you can dig." Some spittle flew from his mouth and was caught in his beard. He sat down. Then, thinking better of it, he rose again, catching his breath over the prospect of what he was clearly about to announce. "I ask—no no, I insist—that you spend a good part of your day seeking out mushrooms. No, not day, not day—night! For you are a precious resource that must be kept veiled safely in darkness. I will account for your harvest and once you meet your weekly quota—well, at that point the time is all yours. You are free to wander and play at will. Now, look at what good Karl gathered in a little more than a day." He lifted a wooden bucket filled with the fungal fruit, some long-stemmed and tree-like, some symmetrical and floral, others bulbous, and a few that were web-like and stringy, like exhumed wedding veils.

"And, my friends—my partners—not a single one of these is poisonous. With something close to supernatural abilities, Karl has completely neglected those varieties that would destroy my reputation as a master mushroomer."

With the dull earthy scent now filling the barn, Gregor realized that they had all smelled these, had been smelling them all along, bursting forth from all reaches of the woods, though only now did they realize the odor's origin. Bodies shivered at the strong scent; heads dropped at the prospect of their new labor. They were once again slaves of the ledger.

"Being a lowly clerk was better," Gregor heard one of his colleagues say.

"Surrounding the forest you know so well is a broader wood, a wood you should feel free to explore, in which you should compel yourselves to use your talents to collect God's gift," Stanko was saying, but his listeners had already turned and started to walk away with dejection. "You will begin tomorrow evening. I have purchased panniers for all of you—here here, let me show you." But by then he was talking to an empty room.

That evening, Gregor went back to Stanko's house and called his name until he came out on the veranda while Gregor stayed behind a hedgerow, not wanting to upset his aunt Helen should she look out the window.

"Uncle," Gregor said, "you are known for miles around as the most extraordinary purveyor of mushrooms. Why do you need us?"

"Because I'm getting old, Gregor, and because we'd like to rest, your aunt and I, and be attended to. The poor woman, even her jaw aches. We would like to hire a nurse, consult a pharmacist. Those godforsaken groans of hers have kept me up for years. I can only pull a kilo or two from the ground each week as things stand. As they stood."

"But you must see that we've already been through so much. To be sent out on labors at night could be dangerous, and there is general unhappiness within the ranks."

"Unhappiness? Look at all the land that surrounds you. Not a being larger than a rabbit to be found for acres, and you have the security of my silence. Why it's a paradise for you, I'd think."

"I can make no guarantees," Gregor said.

"You are free to leave, naturally. I can't say that rumor would not spill down from these hills of a herd of dangerous creatures, the likes of which no human has ever seen. And what of your parents, your poor parents? Shouldn't they be told their beloved son is wandering the countryside, not himself—yes, not himself at all? They are worried about you, and believe that you must be on an extended assignment to the far reaches of the globe. Why, if they knew the truth of it. . ."

So it was that Gregor and his cohort took up the harvest. Stanko was correct that they were exceptionally efficient at the task, and this at first brought a modicum of satisfaction to them. His wagon was stuffed to the brim with baskets and bags of mushrooms as he set out for the market Wednesday mornings. He returned in the evenings red-faced and smiling, a leather pouch singing with coins.

Before long the harvest diminished as the insects shook the woods bare of its treasure. Yet Stanko insisted on his quota, driving them farther and farther away from his estate, into woodlands not his own, across traveled roads, under new-moon nights dark as ink where startled cattle threatened to crush them. Gregor and his friends became weakened, a few even lost a leg or two, but they soldiered on for fear of being revealed, for sheer camaraderie—for one's suffering is diminished when shared with others.

As the cold season set in, and as suspicion grew in neighboring estates that it was Stanko who was somehow responsible for such lowly returns, the former employees of the firm became less and less able to rationalize their plight. They would have to find a solution. Their survival depended on it.

One evening they all stood outside the house, peering in through the dining room window. Gregor's aunt Helen, slouched in her chair, looking downward at her plate of vegetables, seemed to be the victim of a tremor that shook her whole body. Stanko was talking, the dull bass of his voice barely coming through the windowpane. He went into another room and as they watched, the woman raised her head, a big smile lighting up her face. She had been laughing, laughing so hard she seemed from their perspective to be seizing. Now Stanko came back into the room with a long flat box, wrapped and beribboned. She stood quickly, taking him in her arms and kissing him on the cheek.

"You say she's ill, Gregor?" Sasha said. "She does not seem ill to me."

The box contained a new dress of vibrant green fabric, what looked like silk, with a collar of shimmering beads. His aunt stepped out of the room, and Stanko paced back and forth with renewed youth, shaking his head at his new found fortune. Helen returned wearing the dress, and the two began to waltz, sweeping across the living room and into the parlor, then back out again.

"What do you think of *that?*" another said to Gregor, who was himself shocked at the sight, for he'd always assumed his aunt was bedridden. From what he knew, she had been.

"Perhaps she's made a recovery, as he'd hoped," he said.

"Recovered indeed," said another insect. They had all gathered around the window now, and under the moonlight, which was bright enough to cast shadows, Gregor could see how dust and dirt had weathered their once metallic sheen to a sad dullness befitting the beasts of burden they had become.

"Haven't we had enough?" another said.

"Yes, yes, yes," they all said, and waited, all of them, in silence until the house grew dark.

While the couple slept, Gregor's colleagues entered their home, clamoring up the stairs and into the bedroom. After one harmonious and terrible scream, all went quiet. Gregor did not take part in the feast, paralyzed as he was with remorse and indecision. He remained downstairs in the dining room and in the moonlight glanced at a photograph of his mother and father, of his sister Grete and himself—much younger than he was now, but recognizable as a serious boy, a child puzzling to decipher the nature of the moment, a moment captured by the flash of magnesium.

Upstairs, after that one terrible, united scream, he could hear only the sounds of furniture falling over, the clicking and rasping of his colleagues' appendages as they moved about the little bedroom feeding themselves. He hung his head, folded his legs, and lowered himself onto the floor.

When he awoke, all was silent upstairs. He could not help himself, and slowly climbed the stairs.

They were waking up as he stepped into the room, and they were as naked as Adam and Eve, eight men and one woman, humans shivering and feeling their own flesh with the utmost joy, the interminable nightmare over at last. The means of their liberation was also the cure to their physical illness. Sasha lay among them, her slender body pale in the warm glow of the rising sun coming through the windows. She rolled onto her back, bare breasted, clumps of hay, blood and dirt stuck to her skin. Gregor, shocked at the sight, an amnesiac whose memory of beauty was suddenly restored, backed out of the room, but he could not help but peer in from the shadows of the hallway. She opened her eyes and found that some of the men were already staring at her. "Oh," she said, running her hands down her legs with delight, "Oh," her splayed fingers moving across her body. The men looked at her, and she permitted it. "It's wonderful to be back, wonderful." And Gregor knew he would never again be in that house, for upon the bed, utterly reduced, were what remained of his aunt and uncle. Before anybody had a chance to see him, he scuttled down the stairs.

Into the forest he walked, the sun now breaching the horizon, its light gathering around him in flickering shards as he moved deeply into the wood, into its soft darkness and welcoming shadows.

Neutral

Maybe he would get that ride back home, he thought, or maybe he'd have to take the subway. Either way, as he rattled north at a good clip, William was looking forward to being rid of his old friend almost as much as the negotiation itself. Arlene hadn't been explicit about what she was offering for the vehicle, but he had a sense that they'd come to an agreement—*some kind* of an agreement. Already he felt himself unburdened, lighter, *excited.* He realized that buying the car a half-dozen years ago had been an impulsive, semi-stupid act likely intended to fill a spiritual void, one born of urban loneliness amid the din of youthful humanity.

The urge had sprung on him one Sunday night in mid-August, a few days after he'd celebrated his thirty-fifth birthday. As he thumbed through a photo album whose images he was vetting for digitalization, he came upon a picture, circa 1982, of his brother and himself leaning on the hood of their beat-up Plymouth Valiant. He remembered it well: three-on-a-tree, Slant-6, bench seats, a steering wheel with spokes you could squeeze your body through. He wanted to reacquaint himself with that lost world of his teenage years. Of pushing through the gears as the two of them roared around their hilly suburban town—the smell of burning engine oil, blown coolant, a stressed clutch plate filling the air, the whine of the engine echoing off the trees that lined the impossibly dark roads.

After browsing around the web for about a week, he settled on a 1972 Mercedes 220 sedan that was posted on eBay. With its 4-speed stick shift, crank windows, vinyl interior, AM radio, it was your basic tank. He could cruise around the East Village with panache; he could take it on weekend excursions with friends.

The seller was a retired IBM executive from Los Altos, California, who'd driven it to golf outings for the last twenty years and had garaged it its entire life. William knew the car's second incarnation would be less provincial, a bit more. . . punk. For one thing, he'd have to keep it on the streets of Manhattan, a far from hospitable environment.

"When I started off at IBM," the seller wrote to William in one of many email messages that answered his queries, "I was assigned to an office outside Stuttgart. This is when I met my wife. We bought the car about a year before I was transferred back here to California, which is where I'm from originally. My wife was in love with the car and was against leaving it behind, so it came with us when we moved, sort of a favorite pet. It wasn't made for export to the States, which is why it's such a stripped-down model."

Two weeks later the car arrived on a flatbed in front of his tenement like a missile of west coast optimism. The Merc was the pure blue of a cloudless sky. If you could somehow flip it upside down and hoist it a hundred feet into the air on that clear day, it would simply vanish. People stared as the flatbed operator lowered it onto the street. He attached the new license plates and drove it around and around and finally squeezed it into a spot eight blocks away. Jesus, he hadn't given that enough thought, all the driving in circles—rectangles, he corrected himself—just to find free parking in this town.

"To own a car in the city," his dad had said, "you've got to be rich or stupid. And you ain't rich."

He drove the car to Jones Beach on nice weekends with his thirty-something, decent-looking, often hungover friends; or he'd haul himself upstate to his family's Catskill bungalow, which his grandfather Buck had left to William's father. Buck had been an avid hunter and a butchered deer carcass, felled during the Reagan administration, was still entombed in the bungalow's chest freezer.

William had a girlfriend for a while—June, from the Bronx. The car was a key accoutrement of that relationship. They drove as far north as the Adirondacks for weekend hikes. They screwed in the back seat in a parking garage down the block from the Baltimore Aquarium. And they once got stoned and drove down Fifth Avenue, naked, at three in the morning. June liked William for his quirks and physical strength, said she'd never been with anyone as strong and hairy as a bear. "You're my favorite mammal," she would say. As with everything, there was a beginning and an end. She decided to become a registered nurse, which entailed going back to school and then sitting for exams. This was a major undertaking that she'd been thinking about for some time, she said. She'd have to focus "110%" on her studies. He understood. The student loans would be epic, and her parents *and* grandparents were also loaning her money. "Maybe in a few years we'll get back together," she said, "but let's see where we are then." Ah well, he thought, and then began drinking as if the world were about to end.

One afternoon, four years after he bought the car and about a year after his breakup with June, he stood alone in the pine-paneled living room of Grandpa Buck's Catskill bungalow. The place wasn't used much anymore. His brother had gotten married, moved to Vancouver, and started a family. His parents no longer enjoyed the long drive from their Westchester home. Now the coffee table was decorated with mouse droppings and the fire he'd lit was incompetent and sputtering. What little firewood remained was half rotten. Under his feet he could feel the ancient freezer humming in the basement. Through the windows he could see the Merc parked on the wet lawn, listing. He suddenly felt that he was standing for a portrait of representational perfection—this was exactly what his life had become—quaint, hip, stuck in the mud.

He was now contracting himself out exclusively as a technical writer, mainly to banks and insurance companies. Working about twenty-five hours a week, he managed to make ends meet, though he lived on the cheap and his drinking had devolved into a solo sport. He knew he was in a bad patch, his romantic pretenses having given way to the desire for anonymous, feral sex, a desire he had difficulty gratifying and which felt dangerous at times. Yet despite the darkness in his life, there sat his car on the soggy lawn, his constant companion, his horse of another age. The blue was now sun-faded and the roof was covered in a patina of soot and bird droppings. About a year earlier, lumber from a scaffolding truck had spilled onto the hood, smashing in a portion of it. He hadn't bothered reporting the damage to his insurance company. That the vehicle's aesthetic perfection had been ruined meant he no longer had to baby it.

That afternoon he chainsawed a big oak tree that had fallen on the far end of the property years ago. He loaded the thick logs, two or three at a time, into the trunk of the Mercedes and drove them around to the front of the house. The work was messy, with the car doubling as a pickup truck. He split the logs and began a new woodpile under the porch. He worked well past midnight, drinking whiskey the whole time while Hendrix, Zeppelin, the Dead Kennedys blasted out of the house, an old Coleman lamp lighting the scene.

He was so drunk in the end that he could barely make it up to the sleeping loft in the attic. His palms were blistered and bleeding. As he drifted off, he could feel carpenter ants crawling over his face, wearing their little tool belts, going to do their work on the roof beams. The next morning dried blood was smeared all over the place and he was immobilized by the head pain. Apparently he'd come up to the little loft with a second bottle of whiskey, though he had no recollection of it. It, too, was smeared with blood. For more than a moment, he wished he had a pistol to stick in his mouth. On the sheet, next to his face, a couple of big ants were going at a gelled drop of blood like lions at a watering hole. He didn't interrupt them. Rather than move, he urinated in his sleeping bag.

Another year passed, during which a taxi applied a wide em-dash of iconic yellow to the passenger side door and someone smashed in a rear vent window and stole the AM radio. William set a piece of triangular plywood in the window's place. Within a couple of weeks a helpful person had written "♥ window ♥" in glittery silver ink on it.

He managed to cut back on his drinking enough to land a full-time three-month gig creating e-learning tutorials for an insurance brokerage firm in Hoboken. The hourly rate was good and it was a short commute via the PATH train. The routine, which forced him to get up early and leave the city nearly every day, seemed to calm his nerves, lighten his blues. As always, he still had to move the car every night because of parking rules. One evening he found a folded note under one of the wiper blades:

> If we see you driving around the neighborhood drunk
> one more time, you're a dead man.
>
> -Your Friendly Neighbors

Yes yes, he admitted, these people have a point. William always ate dinner before moving the car, and he liked to have wine with dinner, usually a bottle of cheap zin. Traffic and lights were such that he never got the tank past fifteen miles-per-hour. Still, he'd have to change his routine. That night he walked back home without getting in the car, waited a few hours to sober up, then came back and moved it.

Not long after, Lane, a friend he'd met years ago playing ultimate Frisbee down in the East River Park, called. They'd once been close, and Lane, apparently acting as a representative for a number of William's longtime acquaintances, was concerned because nobody had heard from him in almost a year.

"So now that we know you're alive," he said, "tell me what you've been doing with yourself."

"Nothing much other than the new job," William said.

"Oh come on. Last night, for example, what did you do last night?"

"I moved the car then did some still-standing."

"That again? Which pose did you carry on with?"

"A bunch, but mostly the mortality pose," which was an exercise in which, hungry, you stood perfectly immobile, hands at side, toes forward, and stared into an unlighted space—say the dark corner of your bedroom—until you believed you could see your own corpse floating in the middle of the space. The exercise was supposed to alleviate death anxiety and for William it never worked.

"How long did you hold it for?"

"Over an hour."

"Impressive. The only still-standing I do these days is the love pose," which, if William remembered correctly, involved standing fixed in the center of a dimly lit room, slowly *davening*, eyes closed, and concentrating on a person who conjured the idea of pure affection most convincingly. You could use the image of a parent or an early romantic partner, for example. The pose was to be done unto exhaustion and was said to alleviate the pain of loneliness.

"You too?" William said. "I can't find a woman these days because I'm down, and when you're down nobody wants you, which is depressing, and that begets a spiral." He paused. "But wait—you're married. How is Marianne?" He was proud of himself for remembering her name.

"She's in an urn on the DVD rack. You do remember she was sick, that she had cancer? She passed six months ago."

"My God. I'm sorry," William said. "I don't know how I missed it."

"You were on the invite for the memorial. But whatever. People don't expect you to show up these days. Don't beat yourself up."

William realized then that he had an inkling of Marianne's death, a sense of having listened to a voicemail, but he must have been in an altered state at the time.

"I'm sorry," he said again.

"She was always fine being in the moment, you know? Even toward the end she was remarkable like that. I've never witnessed someone so engaged with life right up to the end." This had the ring of memorized, oft-repeated lines. "You could learn something from her."

"You mean by being in the moment? Sure. I've definitely heard that one before."

"I had her on the windowsill and the damn cat nearly knocked her off. *Her* cat. Now she's next to the Coen Brothers. She'd approve—"

"Someone threatened to kill me," William said, changing the subject back to himself, and from death in the absolute to death in the abstract. "They put a note on my car saying I was driving drunk around the neighborhood, that they'd kill me next time." In that moment he realized what a trivial man he had become.

"Is it true, were you?"

"Just to find a spot. I'm not that soused when I take the thing out on the open road."

"One suggestion—why don't you sell that car? You're in love with a hunk of steel."

"It's still got some life left in it, though, and good to get up to the cottage with." He could hear the strange uncertainty in his own voice.

"We'll get some of us together and rent a car," Lane said, "and have a re-union up there. I could sure use it. See, all that driving around you're doing to find parking is no good for you. You're moving in circles repeatedly"—rect-angles, William wanted to correct—"looping back over the same landscape again and again. Eventually life begins to imitate the pattern. Not a man on Earth who wouldn't hypnotize himself by what you're doing."

Rid himself of the old Merc. The idea seemed heretical at first. The car had become his avatar, the personification of his own methodical decay. Yet from the moment Lane proposed the idea of selling it, William knew it was the right—the only—thing to do. June had also once said, years ago, "You've fallen in love with a machine, and that may not be the best use of your energy." Morally, he had no qualms about such relationships. A man could commit much graver sins, after all, than loving a vehicle.

On a hot and dusty Sunday morning in early October, William sat on his stoop, nervously twirling the car keys. After about five minutes a woman in her thirties with dark hair crossed the street mid-block and came toward him.

She wore a tasseled leather jacket, a black skirt worn over black tights tucked into knee-high black Doc Martens.

"William?" she said.

"Arlene?" he said.

"Cool," she said.

They shook hands and began walking east down 9th Street.

"It's a manual tranny, right?"

"Four-on-the-floor."

"I like a good stick. Quick?" She lit a cigarette.

"Hmm," he said. "You have to get to know the gears."

"Fast?"

"Nope. Tops out at one-oh-five."

"Sounds like you know that for sure."

They walked through Tompkins Square Park, past the dog run, through a group of white goth teenagers asking for change. The car was parked on Avenue B under a honey locust tree. She circled it, running her fingers along the inside of a wheel well, a hand along the dented hood.

"Definitely seen some action," she said, throwing down her cigarette and taking the keys from him.

They drove north along the FDR Drive, over the ruins of Bristol, the sun glinting off the East River; they drove over the 59th Street Bridge into Queens, north along 31st Street, and then returned to Manhattan over the Triborough Bridge. At a red light on Second Avenue she put the car in neutral and revved the engine.

"Such a big old boy," she said.

They found a parking spot a block away from his building and it moved him, the way she backed into the spot effortlessly, in one fluid motion. Such grace and precision. He found himself suddenly short of breath, with an erection.

She turned off the ignition and handed him the keys.

"So what do you want for it?"

"Like the ad said. Fifteen-hundred or best offer."

Did his desperate loneliness really have to arrive in this way, at this moment?

"I know that. I read the ad," she said, smiling. Could she see what was happening to him? "Well?" she said.

She waited for his answer, running her fingers through her hair. That she smelled like cigarettes and patchouli didn't bother William. Yet he was unable to speak. "You see, I want the car," she said. "And now having met you, I think we should negotiate further." She wrote out her address. "I'm way up in Inwood. Come over at about eight and bring the registration. And this," and she caressed the steering wheel.

That night, driving toward Manhattan's northern extreme, he wondered if Arlene would offer him a ride back home. The car seemed moodily alive, squeaking and groaning on the bumps and curves of the West Side Highway, complaining in its timid way, invoking the only means it had—springs, bushings, and struts—to let William know that he was alright, that the two of them had wasted a good portion of their lives together, and it was time to move on.

The Suffering of Lesser Mammals

All night Peter had dreamed of carp—of a thousand tenement clotheslines hooked with carp, of kettles filled with carp stew, of carp sizzling in skillets. When he got to the market on Hester Street, the old monger recognized him from days long past when he would accompany his father. With no more than a nod to the young man, the monger lifted a fish out of the great wooden barrel that seemed to boil with activity. For a moment the fish must have thought it had jumped to freedom, for it wriggled in the monger's hands like an apparition, glinting in the sunrise. A minute later, clubbed, scaled and eviscerated, its guts thrown to a yelping mutt, the eyes of the carp remained bright and jewel-like, frozen in that moment of deception.

When Peter returned to the tenement that was his home, he heard the landlady, Frieda Kessemeir, banging on his door five floors up. If not for his relentless dreams, he would have been behind the very door now being harassed in her signature manner. She always carried a large ring of keys with her and used them to strike the doors, a method that was more effective than the fist. He'd thought he had another week or two before it would come to this.

He held the carp now, wrapped in yesterday's newspaper, its flesh cold and heavy, and he stood transfixed, staring at slate steps that rose at a steep angle before him. "Peter Tarkoff," echoed down the stairwell, "open up you little shyster, or out you go." It was not yet seven o'clock, and outside sanitation men were rigging ropes to haul off a horse carcass at long last.

He began to climb the stairs.

Peter's sister and father had both died of tuberculosis. His father, János, barrel-chested and large enough for young Peter to climb like a mountain, died a year ago; his sister, Minnie, who during her short life queried the family with ten-thousand unanswerable questions, two years before that. After his father died, his mother, lost in grief, sallow of face, and suddenly cruel toward him, was taken away to Hartford, Connecticut, to live with her widowed sister, Molly, until she "regained her senses." Molly, who had a small estate from her husband (dead of murder), had been sending Peter enough money to survive, and no more. That had now stopped. He must commit himself to a proper university education if he wished to receive an allowance again, came word from Hartford. "Leave that city of death and learn the ways of educated men," her last letter had said.

He would have none of it. At nineteen years old, he dwelled in the heart of the tubercular beast that had taken his family from him, and he was determined to learn its habits, to breathe its air, to wash its sulfurous smell from his hair. For over a decade the family had occupied the apartment on the fifth floor. He would not abandon it now. He would not leave their spirits behind, diminished as they must be.

Now he stopped between the second and third floors.

"Peter Tarkoff," Mrs. Kessemeir shouted, her voice echoing down the stairwell as she knocked the ring of keys against his door, "you are four months in arrears. Do you hear me you little bastard?"

Peter lived in the apartment above Frieda and her husband, Josef. The couple often fought, and he could measure her daily level of aggravation by the frequency and severity by which her keys sang upon the tenants' doors. Now it was his own door, and the matter was by no means a trivial. The key ring rattled and banged and scraped as she harassed his door. By now most of the apartment doors in the building had gouges on them, as if some great cat had tried to claw its way in.

As he approached the fifth floor, he stopped and hid behind the intervening staircase and balustrade. For years he had observed Frieda with both admiration and fear. Her eyes were dark and drilled into you. *She* was dark, and her provenance was Sephardic. His father had told him that she was born on this very block. He supposed she was about thirty-five years old. Her family had gotten itself mixed up in real estate and this building on East 9th Street had been assigned to her—to collect the rent, to supervise, to inhabit, to desecrate as she saw fit. And so she went about her business of harassing her neighbors, most of whom spoke almost no English and packed themselves tight as kippers into the flats. Though made of iron and brick and stone, the building nonetheless seemed on the edge of collapse from encapsulating so much misery.

"I am coming in now," she shouted. "Do you hear me?"

She slid a key into the lock. "This is your last chance." Then, after a pause, "Very well."

She wiggled and played the key, but the lock would not turn. "You god-damned *goulash*," she said, realizing he had changed the lock.

He thought she would now throw herself against the door and expected an apoplectic eruption. He'd seen how it had gone with other tenants.

But instead she stopped and stood there, arms at her side. Peter watched as she dropped her shoulders in fatigue and leaned forward, sighing and resting her head, with its waxy ringlets of unkempt hair, against his door, the key ring gone silent.

Frieda Kessemeir's small size somehow made her seem physically exacting, a piercing presence in the drab unhappiness of his reality. Her arms had a long reach and her fingers were callused and always working something—a clothespin, a burnished coin, the stub of a pencil. The muscles and tendons of her neck twitched under her skin. The contours of her clavicles, when exposed in the hottest of summer days, were as solid and pleasing to behold as the Brooklyn Bridge. Her facial features were delicate even if her presence was usually menacing. Because of this, Peter was always torn between desire and fear at the sight of her, each made stronger by the other.

Standing in front of his door, her head pressed against the jamb, face looking down, she was muttering and, very quietly, crying. Peter climbed the final steps.

She took her time turning to face him.

"You are four months in arrears," she said, holding the key ring up to him in reiteration, "and you have changed your lock." Her voice softened as she took him in. Beneath his sooty oilskin overcoat his ribs pressed against his flesh and his heart beat like a moth caught in a jar. He saw her husband often in the stairwell or latrine or out on the little stoop, and Peter knew the couple were not getting along. Almost every night he listened to them fight through a gap between one of his floor planks and the baseboard. Sometimes he believed he could hear Frieda strike her husband.

"Come in," he said.

He unlocked the door and they stepped into the small, neatly kept apartment. A bright column of light came through the south-facing window and illuminated some floating cat fur that now spun away. His companion, a nameless mouser that came and went via the fire escape as she pleased, had left her perch on the windowsill and was crouching in the dust and old papers beneath his bed.

"I'll have the rent soon. My aunt promised it. And I'm working."

"Working? Where is the young man working this time?" As Frieda spoke, she started sliding the old apartment key off the giant key ring.

"I'm writing a play."

"A play—you're in the variety show business now? And what is this play about?"

"The needless slaughter of animals we humans seem intent on perpetuating."

"I see. And from this you expect to make a living."

The key came off the ring with an audible snap. She began flipping it between her fingers.

"If you don't give me your rent by this time next week you'll be out on the street, and winter's almost here. And give us a copy of your new key for the ring."

"It's in the kitchen," he said.

He could feel her eyes on him as he took off his overcoat and hung it on a peg.

"You haven't been eating, Peter. Are you sick?"

"It's nothing to worry about, Mrs. Kessemeir."

A copy of the new key was in a glass jar along with a tiny silver pendant inside of which was a daguerreotype of Peter and his sister as child and toddler. He took the pendant out and put it in his pocket, then got the key.

"And why do you never come by anymore for soup, like you used to?" she said from the other room. "You remember?"

"I remember," he said.

"I know how to make soup that you like. When you were a boy we always saved the chicken neck for you and watched you suck the meat off the bones like an old man."

When he came back into the room she was taking in the contents of the apartment with her eyes. If Peter were to die, as members of his family seemed fond of doing, her problems would be simplified, he thought. He imagined her wetting a pencil with her tongue and listing the objects and their value, accounting for his life in her ledger. The furniture, all of it scarred with time, some of it from China and some of it from Holland, and an ornately carved fainting couch in red velvet that was worn bare with his mother's imprint, would be worth more than all the back rent he owed. She would sell it before he was even cold.

The apartment was frozen in time. He could see his little sister tracing the mother-of-pearl inlay of the Chinese bureau, or sneaking behind the writing desk to open its secret drawer that held a tiny coil of paper their father had hidden for them (still present, Peter knew). When his mother was well again and returned home, she would find things as they had always been.

Mrs. Kessemeir knew nothing about the family's cottage upstate. János had wanted a place to take the kids, to show them how to split wood, scythe a field, build a fire—taxing activities he remembered from his childhood in Hungary. He scraped and borrowed until he could buy the old rickety thing, half millhouse (though there was no longer a millstone) and half hunting cabin (though he had not been a hunter). But after Minnie died they visited the place less often. Then his parents had decided that the few dollars it could bring in in rent would be worth the sacrifice. For the last two years the place had been leased to a painter of some notoriety, an ex-boxer named Jonathan Giles. And during the last year he hadn't paid a dime of rent.

Frieda Kessemeir stepped closer and Peter could smell her warm, spicy breath, her scent of dill, onions, and schmaltz.

She dropped the old key on the floor between them.

Peter did not like things to be out of place, and he knelt down to pick it up. While he was on one knee she stepped forward and grasped his head, spreading the strong fingers of one hand on his crown, those of the other on his jaw. She inched forward. "Mr. Kessemeir's not a kind man," she said in a whisper, as if to herself, and ran her fingers through Peter's hair. "He don't care for me like he used to."

She moved closer, his face now a finger's length from her body. She held him as if possessed.

"Please," she said. She moved forward again until the fabric of her dress pressed against his face. The dress smelled, again, like schmaltz and dill, of the privy, tobacco, of the sulfurous, manufactured gas that seemed always to be leaking into the stairwell, source unknown.

"Please," he said, like a mirror.

"Rent's got lots of ways of getting paid," she said, and explained what was expected of him.

That afternoon he cooked the carp whole in a skillet with one onion and two potatoes and some butter. He then arranged the meal on a large plate and removed the head for the cat. Here was that trouble rising up inside of him again. He eyed the headless fish on his plate, seeing its flesh only as the flesh of a once docile aquatic wanderer, a sort of cow of the shallows. He saw it swimming within a dark shoal that moved along a calm inlet. He ate a forkful of the white flesh, forced it down, followed it with potatoes and onion. He ate some more of the fish, capturing the needle-thin bones by pressing the flesh between his tongue and the roof of his mouth.

But before long he was running down the hallway toward the privy. In the darkness of that communal little cubby, the air seemed to be jumping with blue sparks. His neighbors would know it was him retching. Peter, the smudge of a young man, practically orphaned, the sole inhabitant of an apartment that once housed his family. In the air above his head, he could hear flies colliding with each other.

Later, he sat under the gas lamp to write. He felt the ghostly imprints of Frieda's fingers and ran his hands around his face and scalp, the back of his neck, to locate each one. He knew that the tip of his nose, abraded from the fabric of her dress, would have the smallest of scabs in the morning.

A petroleum residue boiled at the base of the gas flame. He held before him a few scraps of paper on which he had scribbled some stage directions, a few lines of dialogue. His play, so far named "The Suffering of Lesser Mammals," was to be no Bowery music show, no triumphal farce. Peter intended to make clear the agony that humans inflict on the myriad animals slaughtered daily for their flesh, all for the simple and blithe enjoyment of men who stained their beards with the fat and blood of innocent beasts. Women were no less guilty, though they carried it off with considerably more charm.

As certain as Peter felt about the gist of his play, he could not get down a single line as he sat there. He knew he would have to go upstate to extract rent from the painter Jonathan Giles, and this thought distracted him to no end. He could find no lease, no written agreement between his father and the tenant. When Giles had first started living in the cottage, Peter and his father would go up and visit. The tenant once described to Peter how to properly break a man's jaw if he were in a brawl. Then he chided Peter, telling him to punch him in the gut. Peter wound up and hit the man. "Your talent lies elsewhere," Giles had said, slapping the boy on the back. At another time he forced Peter to draw a portrait of him using a charcoal pencil. "Oh my. Your talent lies elsewhere, boy," and he'd slapped him on the back. "You'll find your calling and you'll be a fine addition to the male race. I have no doubt about that."

That he would now have to face Giles as a landlord gave him no pleasure. Peter's father would have been the only one in the family capable of putting the screws to the man. But that would have to change. Giles owed him and his mother their due respect in the form of back rent, and he could no longer tolerate life without it. Mrs. Kessemeir expected payment. Soon she would be back to collect the next installment. His father, he remembered, often returned from the trips north exasperated, with a few bills and IOUs stuffed into his pocket. He'd lost his job as a bookkeeper after the panic of 1907 and things were rough, rough right up to the day he died. Before he was stricken he'd taken some odd jobs—whatever he could find. Mostly he was hired as a foreman for work crews digging the trenches for the subways. János was big, he could write, and the men more or less tolerated him.

The next morning Peter took the H&M tubes to Hoboken, where he caught an early train for the nearly two-hour journey northwest to the town of Long Eddy, New York, a few miles from which Giles was presumably still holed up. In the middle of the train ride, around Port Jervis, he opened his leather satchel, lifted out his few sheets of paper, and began working on his play's latest scene. In it, a doctor is examining a young boy complaining of nightmares, vertigo, constant nausea. The practitioner is baffled and prescribes the usual tonics and elixirs he might give to a woman suffering from nervousness—an opium tea and valerian tincture among them. But they do the boy no good. Every night he is wracked with images of bloody slaughters. "For no sleep placates my soul nor provides even a moment's rest whereas demons, who need never rest, enervate me to no end with their torture: they possess me, consume me morsel by morsel." The boy's parents, in response, think him merely sensitive and they worry about him. "I fear our boy is a dandy," says the father one night to the mother, herself an avid lover of mutton chops and veal shanks.

The stage directions called for the parents to always have blood-stained napkins tied around their necks as if in the midst of a never-ending feast. This was the extent of the plot—that the young man was in pursuit of a cure for what he knew was no mere illness, an affliction that ran deep into his soul. Naturally, he was alone in this belief.

When Peter arrived at the village, a center of the bluestone and timber trades, the sun was high and the air crisp, and the wind blew. The Delaware River, normally winnowing its way past the town center with no more than a wrinkle to its surface today gave pattern to each gust of wind that struck it. A small river barge tied to the pier and laden with bluestone was low in the water. Saw logs were gathered together on the opposite bank, clunking into each other. Four men, "rockers," with thick necks and wearing leather smocks pushed wooden carts filled with milled bluestone blocks onto the small pier, where the barge awaited its cargo. They made a line and handed the stone blocks one to the next to the next, the last one then stacked them on the barge. They turned their heads and watched Peter as he walked past them, yet never stopped loading the stone.

The cottage was a three mile walk from the station. Although the encounter with Freda Kessemeir occupied his thoughts, he had other worries to consider along the way. He took a footpath that cut through large wooded swaths framed by rocky outcroppings. The land was jagged and unpredictable, the soil was heavy with clay and therefore not good for much more than dairy farms—though it seemed to grow rocks without trouble. While passing through the wooded swaths Peter felt he was being followed, though each time he turned nothing more than a distant cow or swaying tree was in sight.

He finally caught a glance of a bare elbow sticking out from behind a tree several yards behind him. This person was not exactly stealthy. Peter walked on, annoyed by the theatricality. If he were to be murdered, so be it. Drama comes in many forms, most of them under no control of our own. Finally, he stopped in his tracks and demanded that his pursuer show himself. One of the rockers from the river, short and bracket-like, came out from behind a bower and walked toward him, taking off his cap. Dust rose from the man's crop of short hair. His arms, presumably at rest, were as muscled as an ironwood bough and were raised at a forty-five-degree angle, palms up, as if expecting their next load of bluestone.

"You the boy that owns the place by Basket Creek?"

Peter nodded.

"Well you got a man living there who ain't long for this world if he don't learn how to keep his bollocks in his pants."

"Who are you?" Peter said.

"Mike Wizzen. I saw you get off the train. The constable asked if I could influence you to get your man Giles out of these parts. So I'm attempting to influence you. He's a murderer?"

"They say he killed a man in the boxing ring years back."

"He been knocking around with a local girl that was taken under the wing of the deaf farmer, see. Under the minister's arrangement. And then we stop seeing her at services, and we figure it's the Giles fellow since one of my brothers saw them in the woods a bit too close together not a week ago."

"And what do you want me to do?"

"Kick him out. You're the owner of the place. Get 'im to leave or soon he'll be goin' down the Delaware by no force his own."

The man turned and walked off, and began whistling at some distance.

Soon Peter neared the cottage, skirting the property of his deaf neighbor, the farmer Vendrovsky, who had the odd habit of scything his field well before sunrise and while under the influence of cider. It was now almost noon and sunlight was softening the earth and in some places vapor rose from Vendrovsky's fermenting field. The cut hay, rarely gathered, was lying this way and that and gave off a sweet odor.

The family cottage came into view. Smoke billowed from the chimney and he could see canvases leaning against one another under the sagging porch roof. Some had been blown over. One of the shutters was painted orange. He had sent no word ahead that he would be calling, so he now began shouting hello while still some distance away.

The situation was delicate. Jonathan Giles was known to covet his privacy above all else. No doubt the renowned artist would feel violated at having his concentration broken, his home invaded without warning. As for the rocker's warning, Peter would use it as he saw fit. He looked out over the property. A stand of poplars rose stiff and straight on the distant hill that defined the edge of the property. The population of larger trees closer to the cottage had been denuded over the years: a sick cherry felled and split, a massive maple sold for lumber; another, struck by lightning, sawed off cleanly at its base and split for firewood. The stumps from those big trees, and one massive hemlock stump, a remnant of the tan barking days, had been painted, each its own gay color. The creek was low and shimmering.

As he turned up the stone path that led to the house, a figure appeared and then vanished behind a front window. It was said that Giles often worked in the nude.

When Giles did open the door, he wore a paint-spattered burgundy robe loosely tied around his waist. He seemed to bristle, though he was smiling as well, his teeth as white and square as piano keys. Probably fabricated in Paris, Peter thought. "Well come in, and hurry. The fire is roaring," he said.

The man was tremendous and copper-haired with a pancaked nose and a face that was an agglomeration of ancient traumas. Giles was of an unknown vintage. Of the few events of his life that could be pinned to a timeline, one was that he had stopped boxing after having killed an opponent in 1893 in Yonkers. He had exiled himself for years, spent time in Paris and Brussels and finally returned to New York in 1905. During his exile he began to fall in with artists, who found his "animalism" a stimulating counterpoint to their society of manners. One in particular, a Parisian named Regine Argus, encouraged him to pursue painting and sculpting as an outlet for the aggression he might normally unleash in the boxing ring. It worked for Giles, who, in the eyes of the artistic community, was a primitive, a murderer, and a genius.

The cottage was hot and smelled of paint, solvents, and human labor. But it was only the excessive heat to which Peter objected. He couldn't help wondering if Giles would have built so ostentatious a fire in the hearth if he had split and stacked the wood himself. It was he, Peter, who had labored with axe, maul, and wedge to fill the lean-to. Cherry, maple, oak, other unknown varieties storm-felled and felled by him, dragged through the woods with no love on his part. Alone at the cottage for weeks at a time after his sister had died, leaving his parents to their odd and lonely lives, he'd worked the land hard, cleared the forest of dead wood, blistered then callused his hands on the axe handle.

Again his spirits sank as he contemplated his current situation. Numerous canvases, their backs to him, were stacked and leaned every which way around the main room. Those few that faced forward were draped in fabric to hide their images. Looking out the window, he noticed more colored tree stumps dotting the hills up to where the poplars stood.

"Sit," Giles said. Peter did as he was told and Giles stood opposite him, cinching his robe tighter, and peering at him. "You look like hell, the way the light hits you. I'll make a quick study of you." Here he riffled through papers, sketch books, and stiffened paint brushes until he found a blank sheet of paper and a board to pin it to. He ran into the kitchen and brought out a bottle and two glasses. "This will do the trick," Giles said, filling the glasses, "bring some blood to your vitals." Then, raising his glass to Peter, he said, "To autumn and its inspirations."

Peter looked through the liquor at the distorted image of the spitting fire.

"Well?" Giles said, an edge of his reputed temper coming to the fore. His forehead, an appendage in its own right, was compressed to half its height and looked as if it might spring forth on its own and clobber Peter.

"Yes. . . to autumn and its inspirations," Peter said, raising his glass, then drinking down the liquid in one gulp.

"So Peter Tarkoff has come all this way to check on my well-being."

"I'm always interested in your art, Mr. Giles."

"And well you should be. I imagine that we are a sort of team. It is this—" and Giles held his arms wide to indicate all that surrounded them—"that supplies the inspiration. And it is your generosity that has allowed me to investigate man's tenuous hold on Nature herself."

"That may have something to do with what I observed outside. The stumps. You have painted all the tree stumps."

"It's an attempt to more artfully conquer the land. I assure you that it is only the beginning."

"Mr. Giles, you are presuming that this land is yours, but it is not."

"Nor is the land yours. It is Nature's. Either way, ownership is trivial and fleeting. I presume—I use your word—that it would be your honor to have the name Tarkoff associated with my artistic endeavors, especially at such an early stage of your career. As I say, we are partners of sorts."

"If that's the case, I'd like to know more about your plans. Partners share with one another after all, Mr. Giles."

"Let's start with something you'll understand. I have made a fine portrait of the farmer's daughter, Dahlia. If all goes well, it will be one of my entries at the Union League Exhibition."

He set up a canvas on an easel in the middle of the room. "I've tried to capture her innocence," he said with his back to Peter. "So far from the filth of our native city, you will also see a dearth of sadness in her eyes. She helps the deaf man with his errands, and sometimes acts as an interpreter." Then he stepped out, leaving Peter to contemplate the painting.

If Mr. Wizzen could be trusted, then Peter was not looking at Vendrovsky's daughter, but instead at an orphan entrusted to his care. In the painting she sat leaning back against the knotted trunk of a tree and held a few sprigs of goldenrod in one hand, resting the other on her exposed knee.

Giles may have influenced him with his prologue, but to Peter she seemed as innocent as spring buds pushing up through the soil, and it was true that her expression was unguarded, even inattentive. Giles had captured many fine physical details—the dirt under her fingernails, the calluses on her hands, that she was sunburned. Her face was broad and her hair was hidden beneath a bonnet. A plain peasant blouse, untied, hung off her shoulders as if it were there incidentally, and Giles had limned the outline of her nascent breasts and hips. He had imbued her with the variety of attractiveness usually reserved for Hot Corn Girls in Bowery dives.

The artist returned with a stack of wood and placed it by the hearth.

"How do you find the painting?"

"You say she is my neighbor? I've never laid eyes on her. She looks too young to be Vendrovsky's daughter."

"I say 'daughter' as a turn. She doesn't know who her parents are. I think it's a lonely life for her here, you know. I offer assistance when I can."

The two sat down to eat as the sun was setting. Peter had brought some hard cheese, bread, and smoked fish with him. Giles contributed apples and boiled potatoes and creek water to the meal. Then they began drinking. A few hours later they were still drinking.

"The rent, Mr. Giles, I have come for the rent—that is the truth!" and they both laughed.

By midnight the two were asleep, Peter on the chaise under a moth-eaten wool blanket, and Giles upstairs in the attic. It must have come to that, his sleeping under the roof beams, as the rest of the house filled up with his projects.

The sun had not yet risen when the sound of pebbles striking the roof woke him. Still drunk, his brain adrift in a field of nettles, he began to fall back asleep when from above him in the attic he heard Giles moving around. Then he heard the sound of pebbles striking the roof again and was about to throw off the blanket when he saw the dark form of his tenant slinking down the attic ladder. Giles held a candle as he moved across the floor, blocking the light with his hand. For a few minutes he sat at the table hunched over something before blowing out the candle and donning his heavy overcoat. The sun was beginning to strike the ridge behind the house. Giles stood frozen for a moment, taking in Peter's sleeping form, and Peter saw through his narrowed eyes that he stood there unsure of himself, that something was possibly amiss. His head bowed, he stood stock still for a long time. Then, as if some complex thought process had drawn to its conclusion, he suddenly turned and exited through the front door.

Peter rose and moved to one of the windows. On the other side of the road, not twenty yards away, he saw the subject of Giles' portrait—the girl, Dahlia. It could not have been anybody else. They embraced and then, releasing each other, the two walked off across Vendrovsky's field and into the darkened woods beyond. His silhouette seemed twice the size of hers. Peter, his head filled with nails, was back on the chaise and asleep within minutes.

As the sun broke into the house, Peter saw that Giles had left him a note on the table. "P: a joy, as always. I'm afraid I won't be able to see you off. I will be painting that portrait of you, rest assured! Perhaps we will show it at the Union League. Please buy the following supplies to bring with you the next time you honor me etc.," Listed below were a variety of pigments and their quantities in weight, an amount of rolled canvas, framing supplies, and details regarding a number of paintbrushes and solvents. He gave the name and address of the art supplier, and had added a footnote, an aside: "I have a line of credit with them if you are unable to loan me the funds."

Peter followed a trail made in the morning dew to a work shed located on the opposite side of the field, hidden behind a row of pollarded trees. The shed looked recently built and smelled like timber and tar.

The door was left opened a crack. He could see that Giles was giving the young woman a painting lesson. She sat before an easel, and he stood behind her, his right hand guiding her on the canvas. The painting, though not far along and difficult to decipher, seemed to be of Peter himself, standing next to the cottage and looking back down the road.

"You're better with inanimate things, my dear," he said. "I'm afraid you've made the boy a bit larger than he is in reality. But our little house is well done, as is the winding creek. But the boy can be moved to the edge of the canvas, perhaps here," and he used the back of a brush to mark the spot. "Have him coming or going, one way or the other. I'd prefer him going, to be honest."

"But the painting is no good?" she said.

"You are a beginner, what did you expect? It takes years. Though perhaps this is not where your talents lie," and now Giles took the brush from her hand, placed it on the table, and began to rub her shoulders. She did not encourage him, but she did not protest. "I want to teach you something new," he said, and kissed the back of her neck.

"Not today. The doctor is visiting Father and I need to be there."

"You call him 'father' now? The old farmer's gotten by for this long without you."

"I must though," she said.

"Well then, you can help me and then I will leave."

"No," she said. "I must go. He expects a meal when he visits." She tried to pull away from Giles but he had her by the wrist.

"Please?" he said. "I can't go on not knowing when I'll see you next."

"It ain't natural," she said. "We ought to be together in marriage."

"You know that's impossible," he said. "I could be your grandfather."

"I must go," she said, and before Peter could retreat, Giles released her and she sprung to the door and threw it open before him.

She gave a yelp at the sight of him. "The boy," she said, and ran off toward the farmhouse.

Giles rose but had to re-cinch his belt. Then came toward Peter like a wall, but Peter merely stood there with a smile on his face.

"Now you listen to me," Giles said. "Don't you go 'round telling people what you've seen 'ere or I'll tear you limb from limb like a rag doll." At last, here was Giles revealed. Peter knew he'd never forget this moment. If he survived.

"You must pay me something," he said. "You have not paid a nickel in rent and I am suffering. I cannot make my own rent at home, you see."

"To hell with rent. To hell with comfort."

"You have comfort here, at my expense."

"I have nothing to offer. You can throw me out if you think you're able."

"Pay me something, and I will stay silent."

"I told you what will happen if you peep a word of this. And I don't have a penny to my name. Ain't exhibited in three years."

"Pay me in art then. I have to make my own rent. I cannot lose the apartment."

"Never. You'd sell the piece to the first person who offered you a dollar." Peter turned and started to walk across the field toward the cottage. Giles followed him. "Listen, you are misguided in your stubbornness. Sure, you've had a good bit of tragedy, but family are always fleeting, and it's best to be rid of them before they burden you with their tears, their weddings and their damned coddling. No no, I am envious of you. You are alone."

"I am writing a play," Peter said. This confession slipped from him unintentionally.

"Oh my, a writer. That's something I might have guessed."

Peter stayed at the cottage through most of the day, avoiding Giles, inspecting in detail the color-dappled landscape, going for a stroll around the boundary of the property, and generally taking in the air. He stood for a while atop the hill. Poplars, tall and narrow, swayed in the wind, their branches tapping each other as if sharing a joke at his expense. Almost all signs of summer were gone, and the season of hibernation was beginning. Because the creek was low he could see the undermined roots of several large fir trees that had been planted generations ago along its edge. They'd soon tumble over, he was certain of it.

On the way back through town he left word for Mr. Wizen that he was unable to evict his tenant.

He caught the last train, arriving in Manhattan sometime after midnight.

Peter knew which blocks to take. The Jews had to avoid the Irish and Italians, who had to avoid each other, and everyone had to keep a sharp eye out for the rogue policeman and the drunk brickbatter, both of whom preyed equally on every man or woman.

When he got to his building, he could hear that the laborers on the first floor—about a dozen Poles who'd crammed themselves into one of the apartments—were at it again, fighting and laughing. They were throwing something against the inside of their door—dice, pennies, teeth. He did not know. And the resident gas odor seemed worse than ever. On the fourth floor he stood before the Kessemeirs' door, wondering if he should alert them to the odor. He decided not to. After all, he had no rent money. Then he noticed that rags were jammed under the door, filling the gap.

On entering his apartment Peter discovered Josef Kessemeir standing in the corner of the living room, his unshaven face shiny with sweat, and dirty. He stood on a fixed spot, nearly cowering.

"Why are you here, Josef? Not to kick me out already, I hope."

"I, I have the key. Is how I come in, you see it?" and he did indeed hold forth the single key.

At first Peter couldn't decipher what was happening. Something about Josef, the way he stood, perhaps hiding an object, his eyes jumping around. The apartment was dark.

"Josef? Did you smell that gas in the hall? We must find the leak before we're all asphyxiated or blown to bits."

Josef grimaced and Peter now saw why. He had unfastened one of the gas jets from the ceiling fixture and run a rubber hose from it to a gap between the floor planks and the baseboard that led to the apartment below.

"Where is Mrs. Kessemeir, Josef?"

"Down there, sleeping," and he pointed to the floor.

"You'll kill us all, Josef. Stop this," and Peter moved a few steps closer and saw that one of his neighbor's eyes had been blackened. Josef took a loose match out of his pocket, and more fell to the floor. He sparked the match with his thumbnail and held it close to the floor. The flame lit up his face and he looked at Peter as from behind a dreamy layer. Tears had cut paths through the grime on his cheeks.

"I blow us up." He kneeled and grabbed the hose, threatening to pull it out.

Then he smiled at Peter, who suddenly understood why Frieda might have once loved the man. His grin was full, knowing, and bright—he had the mouth of a millionaire. "No rent for one year," Josef said. "You pay nothing. Nobody bother you, I promise. I take care of it. Nobody notice."

For a moment he was stunned by the words.

But as they took hold his heart raced. He knew that it was not possible that he would let Frieda die below him like that. He remembered her look of weariness, the taut beauty of her face, the determination with which she had held him close to her body. Afterward, she'd told him he had given her pleasure. But already these memories seemed to be taking on the faded tint of the long-ago.

In the silence they could hear the gas as it sped through the tube. The match burned down and went out. The two men stared at each other in the darkness and they listened to the sound of the laborers rising up the stairwell and now echoing up from the street below. They must have opened one of their windows down there. The voices, rough and joyful, full of life and extinguished hopes, filled the air until someone, a neighbor from across the street, told them to shut up. But the racket went on unabated.

Peter would have a year to perfect his play. A year to begin a movement.

A Blintz on Ross 128b

Back when NASA was forced to auction exoplanet rights in an attempt to raise funds for future missions, my grandpa Melvin, a hulking widower with a mischievous sense of humor, bid $2,500 and ended up as the "owner" of Ross 128b, one of hundreds of putative exoplanets that had been discovered indirectly via the wobble of their star's orbit or the fluctuation of their light—or both. Turns out that forty years later, Ross 128b was the best goldilocks candidate within reach of our latest ion engines, its hazy atmosphere—barely discernible through orbital telescopes—rich in the gaseous exhalations of what could well be living creatures.

The planet's size was thought to be similar to Earth's, its distance from its host star closer than we dared to admit, but sufficiently safe given that the star, Ross 128, is a red dwarf. What did that $2,500 buy my grandfather back in the day? A framed certificate whose fine print states that he or an heir of qualifying age and physical condition had won optional passage to the planet should NASA ever send humans there. It was something of a joke. A legally binding one, it turns out.

I'll repeat that: heir of qualifying age and physical condition.

Gramps passed away quietly many decades ago. At the time, nobody in the family had given the slightest consideration to Ross 128b (Ross hereafter) until the good people of NASA discovered that they were legally bound to offer said qualifying heir of dubious physical condition passage on the mission, a mission that would soon be underway. *Offer* passage, let us be clear.

I will say that my fellow astronauts were not thrilled at my decision, at the eleventh hour, to proceed.

"But what will you eat?" was my mother's response when I told her that I'd be among the first humans to colonize a new world. "They say it's going to be a long trip, and I won't have you starving half to death." She wanted to send along some kasha blintzes, her specialty, and one based on a recipe that happened to have been handed down to her from my Grandma Esther, Melvin's wife. Things tend to come full circle in my tribe. Old-world grains plus chicken schmaltz as a means of ancestral continuity, subsequently hurled 65 trillion miles, plus or minus, from Minsk, Esther's birthplace. I'm all for it. But I felt Mother was not understanding the grandness (nay, finality) of what I was about to undertake. I tried to explain that she and my father would be long dead by the time I got to my destination, and that it was astronomically unlikely that I'd ever make it back myself.

"Well, I'm sending some blintzes with you. Let them tell a mother she's not allowed."

As it turns out, we were permitted to bring along "touchstones" from our "home life." So there lay a dozen kasha blintzes at absolute zero for nearly seven decades as I hurtled through space in a windy sleep.

I was the ninth crewmember on a mission designed for eight. My qualification to be on board, as fellow space traveler, triathlete, and M.I.T. physicist Dr. Wanda DeLoach, said, was that I was found in a manilla folder in a rusting file cabinet. But what had I back on Earth but a pile of debt and Anika? Ah yes, but Anika! Anika, who tasted like kimchi and green apples. At least I'd finally managed to abandon her in the manner commensurate with the drama she enjoyed. Leave her for *another planet*. That kind of narrative is a gift to the forsaken. You are welcome, my most aged—possibly deceased— flower.

Locked in a sarcophagus, our bodies' rhythms slowed to a crawl, our cells englassed with tardigrade protein, our skin slathered in evoo, I felt my self— my very soul—vanish into the vacuum of space. In that state of suspended sleep the timeline makes a strange leap from the continuous to the discrete. Somehow, though courting death, you count the beats 'til your arrival at your destination. Loneliness is insufficient to describe that particular abyss. Loneliness assumes you are but a nobody in a universe of people. Here you are a nobody in a universe of nothing. To the one, we each came into consciousness grasping our bundles of supply tubes, as distressed fetuses have been known to hold their umbilical cords in utero.

At first arrival, it seems impossible to comprehend the decades that have passed. The mind claws back time and in vivid cinematic detail projects upon the inside of your eyelids those moments that gave comfort. Stuck in the lander in a tiny sleeping compartment, I was taken back to a summer afternoon a lifetime ago. Anika and I are out for a post-coital stroll down by Hudson Yards in Manhattan, that Garden of Shining Phalluses. As we cross Tenth Avenue, a sports car turns into the crosswalk, nearly clipping my toes and halting in front of Anika, who, with studied grace, raises her middle finger at the driver, pumping it, pumping it. In response, the driver calls her a whore, pulls over, gets out of his car.

I am no pugilist, but I can't recall a happier moment than when the fellow—balding, a hand taller than me, strongly deodorized—shoved me to the pavement in reaction to her offense. Anika stood by rifling her purse in search of cigarettes, as if preparing to watch a dangerous trapeze act. I rose up thinking that nobody dares call Anika a whore other than self on theatrical occasions, and struck this fellow between his square breasts with a right and then a left. God, I was filled with life! The wonder and joy of life! Now I recall that old smell of sublimating asphalt, as if we were heating up the road beneath us. Though of course it was the dying planet. For reference, flies had recently surpassed bees as the primary pollinators on Earth. When I struck him that second time (the left), something gave way deep in his chest with a muffled *click*. It's possible, I now realize, that he had a replacement valve installed, or a pacemaker. Or the entire pump was aftermarket. I swear I didn't know what I was doing. The man gaped at me as if I'd hurled some grave insult. He careered back, and I knew even then that this was a word one gets to use rarely. He fell against his car's side view mirror, which snapped against the chassis, angry. Then he opened the door, tumbled into the driver's seat, and nailed the accelerator, using his indicator before merging into traffic. That gesture of an attentive driver even when under duress told me that this was the sort of person I might have been friends with in different circumstances.

The whole momentous occasion had lasted less than a minute. An unlit cigarette dangled from Anika's lips, and her cheeks were crimson. If she'd looked at herself in a mirror, she might have been embarrassed. But she never did such a thing. We walked on in silence, still heading south. Down the avenue we could see that the wind was wreaking havoc and heading toward us. A dust devil of plastic bags and other refuse was swirling above the traffic, high into the air. Cars were honking at it. What nonsense. As I was contemplating our strange world, Anika turned, looked at me with something like a smile, pulled me into her for a hug, and cupped me.

I could still feel the sharp imprint of her fingernails digging into me as I looked out a pinhole window past the jagged horizon, at our lukewarm star.

By now Anika will have had children, who will in turn have had children. A battalion of cuties lighting up whatever's left of home.

My mission training, being last-minute, covered menial tasks. I was not to be an entire waste of resources after all. Much of my coursework covered chores that would help ensure that we arrived safely at Ross. After five weeks of training I was adept at purging zero-gravity toilets, at changing environmental filters and replacing air lock gaskets. Once on the surface, I was charged with maintaining the generators, draining fuel cells, digging trenches for our sewage, and refilling oxygen tanks. My pressure suit was chalk blue, whereas everyone else's was Space Odyssey white. Supposedly there wasn't enough time to fabricate a suit to my measurements, not to mention a backup suit. Best they could do was to scrounge up a single, tattered training number that would keep me passably alive during the journey. And if not, well I'd be one less mate to worry about, jettisoned. The suit is ill-fitting, baggy around the waist and shoulders, and bunches up around my booties. When inflated, it pinches the groin and neck and cuts off blood to both hands. But it does the trick, I'm happy to say.

Months ago, having finished dusting our little encampment's solar panels, I decided to take a bit of a stroll. In a clearing at the bottom of a shallow crater that provided some protection from the wind, I spied Dr. DeLoach— Wanda—bent over her charge of seedlings, whispering to them. Willing things to life in an inhospitable environment wasn't even part of her official duties, but this is who she is. At the sight of her, my heart went a-fluttering. You try to find love—you say the word over and over to yourself, you remain attuned to its symptoms. But in the end you follow the script, pursue bodily pleasure, and happily call it a day. For people like me, the fear of loneliness is not as paralyzing as it would be for a deep-feeler, a sentient, full on *mentsh* who understands what it is to be in the company of his fellow humans, who yearns for their warmth, their scent, who finds companionship—deep companionship—necessary. Though I have grievances like all my countrymen, in the loneliness department I'd always considered myself half a man. After all, when you convince yourself you can survive without love, you can survive without love.

Yet here was Dr. DeLoach. Wanda. Seeming to undo all that. The scrim of desolation through which I'd been viewing my life was suddenly revealed to me. Who stood in the way of building new relationships, of proving myself worthy? I did. And my ridiculous, humiliating blue pressure suit. Even in that thin atmosphere, you could hear the *zizzing* of my thighs as I approached my fellow pilgrim.

To place this in the timeline, we'd lost Al Hayward and Joyce McCallan a few months earlier. They'd gone to reconnoiter the ancient river delta—our intended landing site—but hadn't returned. After a few weeks of silence, and no luck at all from their location beacon, we wrote them off as kaput. The crew was getting smaller and more nervous even as we were making progress in expanding our local footprint.

We knew that the air was nearly breathable, needing but a supplemental kiss of oxygen. We also knew that the temperature, ranging between zero- and sixty-degrees Fahrenheit, was entirely doable. Yet during the first year of our occupation we were required to remain sealed inside our suits while outdoors. Rendell and Pierson, our biologist and chemist, respectively, were spending every waking hour running a battery of tests on our virgin environment to establish ecological and atmospheric baselines. The main offense we could commit by disrobing outdoors would be to destroy a vibrant civilization of sentient beings via contagion. That seemed unlikely. The place was essentially a desert, from what we could see. Second most offensive would be to destroy an ecosystem of less intelligent beings—presumably those unseen by the naked eye. I was taken to understand that Rendell had discovered the existence of a spectacular bacillus, structurally similar to what you might find back home, but with flagella that had evolved into little rotary blades; that is, the damn things could *fly*. Third most offensive act would be to get ourselves killed by toxins or biological predators against which we had no defense.

Thus the pressure suit requirement until we were able to sort out every last detail. Thus the ultimate frustration of my life, approaching a fellow human being on a bright-ish afternoon and wanting nothing more than to feel a bit of skin against mine, to smell her breath, yet to have a pair of impenetrable barriers between us. The crew was only now beginning construction of our more permanent shelters, enclosures that would allow us to undress without bumping our elbows into graphene panels, homes designed, I presume, so that the crew could eventually reproduce.

So then, back to Dr. DeLoach.

She was in her fabulous, well-tailored pressure suit, and with quilted twee-zers was massaging a sterile clod of pampas grass she had germinated from seed. The blades were droopy, brown-tipped, and this worried Wanda. I in-ferred disquiet from her stillness as she squatted before them, head cocked to one side, glass visor steaming up a bit. Her back was to me, but I knew the flapping and crinkling noises produced by my space bag had alerted her to my approach. The last thing any of us wanted was to inadvertently scare the crap out of a compatriot. A sudden spasm of fear, a micro-breach in a pres-sure suit seal, and suddenly the entire experiment is over. I reached a shaking hand toward her, but let it hover there, inches away from what would be, in regular nature, her thick hair resting on her dark shoulder, her adorable ear with its intimate whorls. I withdrew, grunted, most definitely alerting her to my presence. Nothing. Then I noticed some movement within her helmet, her face and jaw spasming slightly. Aha, she was listening to tunes! Music outdoors while on the clock—this was not allowed. I'd caught the good doc-tor being a bad doctor. Of what else was she capable?

That face of hers, when free and clear of the rhomboid enclosure, was spectral and welcoming simultaneously, as if she could see both the enzy-matic reactions that made you love her, and the poetic impulse they would generate. She was incisive, too, the first to realize a mascon—that is, mass concentration—lay beneath the planetary surface as we made our harrowing entry, causing a dangerous perturbation in our trajectory; and she was the one responsible for picking the emergency landing site in less than thirty seconds. The disrupted descent had disturbed her greatly, as if Ross were dead set against us, and here we were forever in its igneous grasp. Now, too, that spectral face of hers showed signs of distress. In a word—one that has an entirely different weight out here—she seemed worried.

I backed up, swiveled on my booties, and continued on to my scheduled task, checking the lander's No. 2 heating coil, which was behaving a tad er-ratically. Before we lost Hayward and McCallan, the tiny escape pod within the lander was my home for the same reason I had the blue suit: I was an addendum. But with the loss of my crewmates, I was given their modest dome-like home (we call them "interims"), though I was still on my own. The lander, however, remained a great resource for anybody in the field, a garden hut-garage-outhouse combo to which we could retreat on our breaks, seal ourselves in, and strip to our skivvies.

While I was still outside under the lander checking the coil connectors, I heard DeLoach singing to herself in the thin atmosphere. The voice was eerie and tinny and full of loss: fresh, human, and alive. I swear I felt the ground shift beneath me. The tune was Patsy Cline's "Crazy." This was a sound I'd never heard, because none of us had ever broadcast our naked voices out on the surface.

To wit: she had removed her helmet.

Now the good doctor was being extremely bad, was jeopardizing the whole reason we'd sacrificed our lives to this distant world. I watched her, hidden behind some mafic boulders. She ran her fingers through her hair, inhaled deeply through her nose—a yogini no doubt—and then refastened her helmet, exhaling within its confines.

She was moving my way, heading for a break in the lander.

"You're on your back a lot these days, Edmund," she said, coming upon me.

"So much to do around here, and not enough time to take in the air," I said.

"Anything I should know?" indicating the lander.

"One of the heaters is out. It'll be a bit chilly in there. I'll have it fixed in a jiff." For reasons unknown at the time, electrical connectors shimmied out of the lander's underside now and then, or lines would break entirely in the middle of the freezing night.

"Much obliged," she said, and she opened the lander's hatch, vanishing inside with a click and the hiss of the venting airlock. The moment she disrobed, the lander would be compromised, ruining the one place, other than our little interims, we could find solace. And I was too shy, or too engorged, to stop the contamination. I could feel the lander creaking overhead as she moved about. Gravitational effects are intimate, I've come to learn. Back home the creek of a floorboard was annoying, something to mend. Here it is a reminder that our lives are not illusions, that the best- and worst-looking of us are equally adept at tumbling down a flight of steps. But even more so around here. Because over a mascon, gravity is a fickle jokester. Bubble levels are useless, for example. One feels an intuitive unease, as if stuck on a subway making a long, slow turn in the darkness. I heard the hard *thunk* of DeLoach's helmet hitting the floor, as if tossed off with abandon, followed by the soft patter of her feet, the trickle of water going through the lines, pulling from the purification system, then heading the other way, pumping out waste to same.

An hour passed before I finally finished the repair, and Wanda had not yet emerged. I headed back to my keep to settle in for the night. There, the wind kicking up beyond the ridge and whinnying into the darkness, I did my crunches, downed a thimble of corn whiskey, and ruminated.

Though I figured it was not reciprocal, I had a sense of a growing bond with Wanda, an affection both deeper and broader than a mere crush. This is a woman who could have run the mission on her own, who wanted to establish an entire ecosystem of flora and fauna, but who, instead, was now exposing all of us—and potentially all of *them*—to who knows what. As mentioned, we'd already lost Hayward and McCallan. Literally lost them. Their location beacons stopped pinging and we could see not a trace of them from the high ridge, even with infrared scans.

Ross was not a cruel planet, but neither was she welcoming. Dr. Rohan Feng, our mathematician, was working on proving a hypothesis that he'd posited based on the timing of gravitational anomalies, that Ross has a dual core, a dense iron core rolling around the interior of a less dense composite core.

Feng explained this to us one morning in the mess tent. "Think of the inner core as a lead-filled ping pong ball rolling around the inside of the outer core, a cream-filled basketball, itself rotating within the center of the planet, a beach ball." First light was arriving, and we were throwing down instant oats and, it seemed to me, itching to get outside. Feng had been working all night, his voice shaking. "And imagine here we are on the surface of the beach ball minding our business. When the lead-filled ping pong ball passes deep beneath us, well, that's when we feel the effects of the mascon."

Dr. Reshma Mahendru, our MD, chimed in, explaining that the sudden increase and fluctuations in gravity could cause inner ear issues, such as nausea and disorientation, and, on rare occasions, disinhibition or worse. As more episodes came to pass, Dr. Feng planned to fine-tune his model until it became predictive.

Now I understood why Wanda had taken off her helmet. She'd had a moment of not giving a damn. Her true self had poked through the carapace of genius and solitude.

Weeks more passed in relative harmony. I kept zuzzing around in my misfit suit doing my chores. I'd managed to set up the coffee machine in the lander so that the water reservoir auto-filled. While Zeno Hickman, our systems designer, was managing to excavate for, and assemble, our entire future village, including sewage treatment plants, solar panels, a comms station, and observation tower; and while Feng was fine- tuning his core-within-a-core predictive model, I was spending my time affixing a little plastic float valve to our coffee machine's reservoir. Meanwhile I was pretty sure that Dr. Mahendru and Dr. Feng were boning. It had begun at last. Procreation.

I began to note that whenever I was under the lander (not an infrequent event) Wanda would happen by and step into the vehicle, thudding around in a manner that I began to suspect was demonstrative. Beneath her, looking up at the lander's intimate underworkings, I could only imagine what she might be up to within it. One afternoon we were repeating the usual ritual, Dr. DeLoach caressing her pampas fronds (the plants now flourishing) while I was pitched under the lander on my back. In this instance it was legit—I was installing expansion joints on all the fittings. Feng had told us to brace ourselves for the next gravitational disruption in the coming hours, a timeframe that corresponded nicely to what I hoped would be a regularly scheduled drive-by by Wanda.

Happily for me, at the appointed time she meandered down the worn and gritty path toward me, and you could already feel the strange pulling sensation of the approaching inner core. In the right mindset it was stimulating, an all-encompassing weightiness, a planetary hug.

"There he is, the hardest worker around," she said, cheerily enough. "Got any updates?" I'd already embarrassed myself by mentioning the miraculous coffee maker auto-fill valve to the crew. I sat up, put down my tools, and said, "Nope. Other than I'm happy to see you."

"Is that so? Don't tell me you're getting sentimental, Edmund."

"I wouldn't call it that," I said.

"Well what would you call it?" She had her hand on the railing and was about to take her first step up the lander stairs.

"I don't know. A bit lonely."

"You mean you're a human being like the rest of us? I'm glad to hear that."

From my vantage point, and because I was aware of the timing, I could see the lander list slightly to one side as the inner core began passing beneath us.

"What do you do in there anyway?" I asked.

"Oh, this and that." She was lingering, running her gloved fingers along the railing.

"I'd like to join you in there," I said. When you're encased in a space bag and helmet you revert to unembarrassed proclamations.

Wanda turned a full 180 degrees to face me. "But that's against protocol," she said, "both of us inside at once."

"Not if we stay in our suits," I said. I started putting away my tools to move things along. I went about it very slowly.

When I finally stood up, she gestured for me to follow her up the steps.

"I know you took your helmet off out here," I said on the way in. "I don't blame you."

"Well then I guess we're ruined anyway," she said, and sealed the door behind us.

We have since tried our best to time our rendezvous to the cycles of the inner core. Making love when the sphere of molten iron is beneath us seems to amplify the act, maybe because it's more taxing. Even now I can't figure out why Wanda took an interest in me. At first I thought, with a bit of guilt, that her willingness had been symptomatic of disorientation, the epic inner ear issues Mahendru had predicted. Why else would Wanda hop in bed with the itinerant from the rusty filing cabinet? But as our assignations continued, I stopped asking the question. Likely she just likes a guy who can fix things around the house.

One afternoon last week, the inner core having released us from its grip, Wanda and I lay on our sides staring at each other among the tangles of wires and laminated user guides strewn about the lander floor. As she often does during moments like these, she stared quietly at me, seeming to scan my face for any signs of happiness. Often she finds a scrap. She wants me to rise to every occasion, and I do my best.

"So what did you take with you all this way from home?" she asked, which is the most intimate question one far-flung traveler can ask another.

"Some kasha blintzes," I said. "My mother's specialty." I expect neither sympathy nor understanding regarding my choice.

"Kasha? I love kasha." I hadn't expected that. I suppose Wanda was being polite. "They're in the nitrogen freezer?"

"Right over there," I said. For those of us who'd brought along perishable memories, the squat cabinet under the bulkhead was all that stood between us and oblivion.

"Can we have one of them?" she asked. I was a little taken aback, to be honest. To consume a portion of my touchstone was to eat a fraction of my soul. Then again, my mother would be happiest if I were to share the meal with a nice girl. Even a shiksa would be okay if you're far from home.

Then Wanda added, with a sly smile, "I happen to be extremely hungry. You see, I'm eating for two."

Well okay, I thought, and stood up, naked. I looked over at our pressure suits crumpled in the corner—one blue, one white. I felt as if I'd molted. The next time I donned that thing I'd be a tad more serious. A baby, in this place? My baby, *ours.*

I'll have to figure out what to tell the little tyke, explain my part in bringing it into this world. Let's hope I can conjure a narrative that carries the kid through the hard times, because we're without precedent down here, without history. Without, until Hickman gets to it, a playground.

I offered my hand to the good doctor, pulled her to me, and together we took the half dozen steps to the freezer.

The Coastal Shelf

Peering up at a dense stand of sequoias from the porch of his rented cabin in Big Sur, Andy Minter burst into tears. Nature was marketed as the universal salve, the fixer of high blood pressure, the relaxer of vertebrae. But for Andy it demonstrated a void impossible to fill. The sweet air reeked of isolation and dread, despite complementing a beauty so profound he found himself laughing (before crying). There he was, laid out on his back in the early afternoon, drunk, and he was bawling like a child. His life came into focus. It was nothing but a blank piece of paper. And someone had tossed the pencil in the trash. He managed to rise, leaning against the porch railing, and let his face fall into the crook of his elbow, hugging himself under the purple-blue sky. Tears caught in that crook wetted his forehead.

He'd flown out to Mountain View to partake in compliance training required by his employer and had decided, now to his chagrin, that he'd tack on a couple vacation days, rent a convertible, and drive south on Route 1, taking in the Pacific views he'd heard so much about. He'd always wanted to see Big Sur, to pass through its mythical air, but hadn't expected himself to become such a wretch in its midst.

Back in his Hell's Kitchen apartment thirty-six hours later, he flipped open his laptop and out rose a drowsy cloud of gnats, stowaways from that impossible land. Apparently while he'd mourned for himself in the rustic cabin, they'd settled in his keyboard, attracted to the machine's warmth. And there they remained—for his drive south to Los Angeles, the flight east to JFK (may have shifted unexpectedly in overhead bins), through traffic on the Van Wyck Expressway, and finally as he climbed the stairs to his apartment. Thrust into the living room on that fall evening, they briefly swirled about in a tiny congregation, then dissipated into the dark corners like lint.

At around the time of Andy's episode in Big Sur, a different sort of crisis was unfolding a mile south of his New York City abode. During the construction of a new pier on the Hudson River, a pile driver slamming its charge a foot at a time into the riverbed silt suddenly found no resistance, and the steel pile, of its own unimpeded momentum, slipped the machine's grasp, vanishing beneath the water's surface with a hissing sound. The Hudson emitted a few bubbles, and then a whirlpool began forming. The steel pile had apparently pierced the riverbed and penetrated an ancient void beneath. As the construction crew scrambled to unmoor the barge and cranes and move them into open water, a crowd gathered along the adjacent bike path. Cars soon blocked the southbound lane of the West Side Highway, then more rubberneckers blocked the northbound. Before long the penetration expanded and mist rose from the whirlpool as if from rapids, the roar of rushing water audible from several blocks away.

Soon the construction workers who'd escaped massed along the riverbank behind a chain link fence, chatting into their phones, trying to conjure the scene they'd witnessed, heads bowed. The news showed images of these women and men, day-glo safety vests lit up in the setting sun, still wearing their hard hats as if the sky might fall.

Andy had found success in life, and he could prove it. He used an app for his laundry service, summoned limos nearly to his stoop, and had his meals delivered to his apartment door as if he were a person with mobility issues. Recently he'd had a bump in salary and had implemented what he considered the ultimate luxury—setting his credit card to autopay. What did he have to show for his work, his multifaceted success? A lot of cashmere sweaters that he stored in a cedar chest, which he called his coffin. To be both materially comfortable and entirely rudderless was not a complaint he could voice aloud. He enjoyed himself when he could, and despaired only when required—and always in secret. The one solace in his life, other than bouts of sex that were sometimes totally awesome, was swimming. The gym complex down the avenue from him had an Olympic-size pool. On weekends he'd do the crawl for hours, until the local SCUBA class kicked him out. Swimming was medicine taken in crisis, a means of exhausting himself physically in order to beat his mind into submission.

The night after his return from California, Andy shaved, showered, cracked a beer, and called Alyson, his favored lover. Within thirty minutes they were in bed together. Within forty-five they were drowsing in each other's arms. She rested her face on his shoulder, cleared away her auburn bangs so that he could see her eyes, green and sparkling gem-like under the bedroom's LEDs. She ran her finger around the fuzz of his ear's helix. To him it sounded as if a jet were passing overhead.

Then he took her hand by the wrist and pulled it under the sheets, urging it down.

"Don't be a jerk," she said. "Use words, okay."

"I'm sorry," he said.

Andy suspected that he fit the profile of a certain contemporary type to a T: the unimaginative and presumptuous urbanite living in the secular universe, willfully ignorant of the millennia of ancestral suffering that had brought him to this point in time and space. What could he do to counter this impression—how could he kill the trope, prove he was an original? Whatever he might try had already been embraced by everyone else in his demographic: tattoos, piercings, molly-gobbling. How would he differentiate himself? What was his *brand*? Had his father—a real fan of Andy's so-called success—ever had a brand? Alfred "Freddy" Minter was an accomplished civil engineer in his own right, had infused Andy and his two sisters with ethics and a love of the natural world, and probably would not have a single regret in the end. Unless Andy became an abject, violent, arsonistic son. Always a possibility. And his mother, Natalie née Palachnik. She'd started off as a homemaker. Stressed out and dish-shattering, she'd gone back to school and earned, after nearly a decade, a PhD in psychology. In the early aughts his mother started a private counselling practice in the family's house, a practice still going strong. Back then, Andy would return from college on holidays and find a note on the front door directing him to enter the house through the basement, meaning his mother was seeing a patient in the family's living room. Once in a while he'd hear weeping behind the closed and heavily curtained French doors, followed by a long silence and then, finally, a car starting up curbside and trumpeting off into the distance. His mother would open the French doors, take a breath, step across the threshold into the dining room, and say, "Anybody else need a cup of tea?"

The patients' vehicles were usually compact numbers, four-cylinder engines, rattling fenders, dangling tailpipes, manifestations of their tripped-up drivers. Andy had once recommended to his mother that she check out their cars before calling her patients to the couch. One summer he'd even volunteered to wash the vehicles as she did her work on their owners, allowing them to emerge from therapy with at least one tangible improvement, a shiny carriage waiting to take them home. Nothing had come of it, but he'd garnered a laugh at the dinner table—a rare feat. Anyway, she, Natalie, his dear mother, was certainly not in need of any branding. She was foundational to his life, secure in her mission, never doted on him or his sisters. She'd been there from the get-go as a beacon of what a silently determined person could become. Where was *his* beaconhood? How might *he* impress the world with his labor?

Blue dye was released into the Hudson, adjacent to the whirlpool. A waiting fleet of volunteer boaters were poised to spot its reemergence in New York Harbor, the Long Island Sound, Poughkeepsie, or anywhere, please. Its reemergence never occurred. Radio trackers were released into the abyss, the signals fading fast, dropping to several hundred feet, then ceasing. Tethered cameras were placed on rafts then allowed to plummet into the depths. They sent back images of blackness, bubbles, flashes of light, but found neither solid floor nor directional current. Cables came back *sans* cameras, ends tied off in neat knots.

He'd returned from Big Sur on a Thursday night, and Alyson left him alone again the following Saturday morning. But not before taking a long shower and filling his apartment with modern day esters—the scents of sandalwood and fruit salad—and beneath it the baseline smashed-grass fragrance of her effusive person. After she left, Andy considered his course of action, his escape from cliché and mundanity.

Two weeks passed. The West Side Highway reopened, the Department of Transportation having installed a temporary barrier to block the view of the angry whirlpool. Still, tourists swamped Andy's neighborhood, walking west to the river to selfie their way down the esplanade, to get as close as they could to what was now being called the Chelsea Sink. From his building's roof he saw mist rising up in a column a mile south, drones speckling the sky above like flecks of pepper.

The National Oceanic and Atmospheric Administration had discovered that coastal waters had receded. The Army Corps of Engineers was contracting heavy equipment on both banks of the Hudson; dredges, tankers, and wildly instrumented ships were spotted in New York Harbor. Some, with gantry cranes akimbo, made their way north when the tide came in. They were to build a cofferdam around the sinkhole to hold water back from the void, though this was the very sort of action that had caused the problem in the first place. The Navy had taken an interest, too, and moored an obelisk-like battleship within plain sight of the trendiest restaurants in the Meatpacking District. If an alien vessel were to rise out of the misty void, America would be ready.

Andy decided to have a side part etched into his hair with a laser, disabling a fine line of follicles that had served him well. The part was as straight as a jetfighter's wing and demonstrated an attention to detail impossible to conjure by any other means. And Alyson, it turned out, was pregnant. By a process of elimination, she was certain the child was Andy's. She broke the news to him at a local coffee shop late in the morning. Sun was bursting through the cafe's glass facade, shadows from passersby flickering across their tiny table.

"You're okay?" she asked, as if he were the one carrying the child. "You do want to keep it? Not that it's your call. But it would be nice if. . ."

"Of course," he said, gripping her hand. If they weren't in such a quiet place he'd have shouted it. Later, he wished he had done just that. The child would be awaiting sage advice from him. But he'd have only one line to start things off: I'll do my best. Which was always his line.

Cross-checking his diary against the news, Andy discovered that the puncture beneath the Hudson occurred at about the time of his Big Sur eruption. That tearful slumping in the primordial bower had come over him so quickly, seemingly without reason or warning. Might he have been in touch with something larger than himself? Perhaps he was not merely a standard-issue, feckless human after all. Maybe he was an attuned Druid who'd felt the piercing of the Earth. Even more so, maybe his despair was so great and so penetrative that he'd caused the wound.

NASA soon noted that the moon was moving into a more distant orbit, foot by foot. It seemed that the water entering the Sink was leaving the planet entirely, sluicing into an unseen dimension or spraying into space like some angry ejaculation. The Earth was losing mass, and was flinging the moon further afield. Experts argued about whether this loss of mass was sufficient to disrupt the Earth's orbit around the Sun. Which raised the unthinkable thought: would our lightening planet move further and further from its life source, heaved into the frozen hinterland?

Where was the panic? Andy could not be the only one losing his mind. If nothing were done, the void would finally be sealed only when the Earth's water, what remained of it, froze solid, and the planet's atmosphere came down atop its billions of corpses, like snow. On the other hand, *he was going to be a dad*. What kind of dad would he be? Resourceful, sure. Handy, no doubt. But capable of moral guidance? Of lovingkindness?

Branding was all about nouns. Andy needed *verbs*.

For years he'd kept an inflatable dinghy in the cubby above his bedroom closet. If things got terrible, had been his thinking, he could toss the craft into the Hudson and paddle to New Jersey—and the mainland. Now he pulled it from its cocoon and unfurled it in his living room. The apartment filled with the evanescent odor of exposed vinyl. The pump worked, the seals held, the vessel balancing on his coffee table like a kind of joke. He deflated it, jammed it back into its cocoon, and hauled it to the river, dragging the paddle and pump behind him. Nobody out on the streets seemed to give a toss.

South of the Intrepid Sea, Air & Space Museum, north of the Circle Line pier, he jumped a steel railing, lowered the dinghy from the rope on its bow, clambered down, and knelt into it, pushing himself off into the night. As he paddled from shore, the hum of cars on the West Side Highway first grew louder, echoing off the wall of buildings that lined the roadway, and then, at about two-hundred yards out, ceased entirely. All at once it was dead quiet.

Flood lights shown in the distance, and vibrations pushed up through the vinyl membrane of the dinghy, the churn of heavy generators. Soon a plastic boom bobbing in the chop came into view, giving shape to the water's surface. He'd seen it in daylight necklaced around the Sink. It demarcated the point of no return, he supposed. Then the low beckoning pitch of the whirlpool itself came to him, an insistent white noise lulling him into a state of dim denial. Leaning into each stroke, he dipped the oar deep, heaving himself forward. He would make a wide arc around the periphery, get to know the anomaly for himself, commune with it in the same way he'd wanted so desperately to commune with the sequoias in Big Sur.

Passing over a dense tangle of refuse, the oar snagged and was yanked from his grip. He fished for it, elbow- then shoulder-deep in the water, searching among the flotsam of the city. It was gone. He began to paddle with his hands, but had little success. The dinghy was soon being pulled toward the boom.

Earlier that day Alyson had had him install a pregnancy app on his phone so that he could track their offspring's development in her womb. "Perfect for you, this one," she'd written. Possibly she was being ironic. While the more popular apps matched the progression of a fetus to fruits and vegetables of similar volume—grapes, kiwis, eggplants, and the like—this app was intended for "people in the trades." The embryo was currently the size of a 12mm socket, but he'd already swiped through its stages, watching it grow to the size of a fuel filter, sprinkler valve, onward to engine piston, plumber's torch, and, finally, coil spring. Their child was apparently a creature of utilitarian contrivances, but it was the only valuable thing Andy had produced.

Now he stared at the phone in the darkness as the dinghy rotated in the current. Alyson had texted him several times, sensing that he had not processed his burgeoning role, the mutation his schedule was to undergo. Her final text, sent a few moments ago, said, "Don't do anything idiotic. We'll be great."

Yet she hadn't tried to call him. Not even once. If she were concerned about him, might that have been a better option?

The little vessel was now riding over the boom. Should he leap, and swim for it? To witnesses along the riverbank, including encamped media personalities, he'd claim a narrative of daring and guts, and certainly his close call with the Sink would make the news. Or they'd see him as a crazy wanker who couldn't manage the basics of paddling. On the other hand, if he stayed where he was, he'd be transported to another realm entirely. For the first time in his life, he'd have made a solid decision, one of self-cancellation. Then again, wasn't the simplest solution usually the best? Meaning, he should stick around, if only for the kid. He began a short text to Alyson. "Hey! I'm totally fine—" and then he was swallowed up.

Bring on the Happies

Just out of the shower, a puddle forming at his feet, Vernon stood in his kitchen staring down at his laptop screen. Staring back up at him were his cookie lists. Column after column of them, row after row of alphanumeric hashes: the depressives and addicts, the self-mutilators, onanists, jihadists; the shooters, snorters, and sounders—all waiting for something better to do with their forsaken lives.

The apocalypse is already upon us, he knew, having arrived the Thursday before last, or thereabouts. The End was not a discrete event for which one could pack a bag as if going to a picnic. No, it is wily and gaseous, and has already set itself down right under our schnozzes, and we barely got a whiff. Fact is, we're in the midst of it *right now*, Vernon thought, and in its wake humans will be that much more depleted and unbearable. He did not subscribe to the timeworn tropes of black helicopters, zombies, truncheons, and sarin. The current situation was even more terrifying: the diminishment of camaraderie and wit, the collapse of truth, a fit of dyspepsia that has no end. That little drop of blood he'd spotted in the toilet earlier this morning was but a prelude.

Though he was no fool. He was bracing for violence born of ignorance, amplified by fear, realized by firearms.

True, the buses were still running up Tenth Avenue, subways trundled along beneath the estuaries and thoroughfares of the boroughs, and jetliners etched their contrails across pink sunsets. But shot through it all was the indisputability of the end of civilization, the death rattle of humanity. What we need to do now, he thought, is make our way in the post-apocalyptic morass.

But who among our community will be our allies? With whom do we want—in all likelihood—to die?

He was alone, despite his revelation. Alone, even though he was sur-rounded by thousands upon thousands of the very people with whom he believed he should hobble across the finish line.

Those special misanthropes he'd become adept at identifying on the web—the souls looking up at him from the begrimed laptop screen—were, like him, hunkered down in their grottos, from Astoria to Whitestone. They were crying into pillows, screaming into empty closets, shooting into sheets of Brawny: seeking bloody pleasure and pain as a salve for the broken-down world. Others were learning how to tap and thread pipe, stashing fertilizer in their storage lockers.

The laptop's cooling fan kicked on and whirred up to speed. In his pres-ence the lists were becoming spirited, antsy.

What if he were to work a miracle and transubstantiate these bits of text into human beings, birth them with a wet splat onto the parquet floor of his apartment? He would serve them drinks and canapés, put on some Coltrane and Ramones, test their mettle with Throbbing Gristle. He would see what they were all about, these future heroes.

Vernon had spent the first part of his career pushing browser cookies through ad serving pipes to help luxury brands sell their shiny wares. It turned out that he had an innate ability to pinpoint the particular combination of online habits that sang of wealth. To those people whose cookies he had captured in his net, brands would serve ads that would downright tickle their groins with commercial desire. And at a price to advertisers that brought a great deal of pleasure to Vernon's boss at the Greyville Agency—and a hefty bo-nus to the conjurer himself. This sort of success had been no small feat as the first decade of the new millennium wound down. Consumers were be-coming either blind to or enraged by the flashing, animated, shouting banner ads that harassed them minute by minute, that followed them around the web like an adolescent crush.

For Greyville he had created thousands of audience lists with titles such as "Yoga Enthusiasts," "Soccer Moms," "Weekend Warriors," "Bible Thumpers," "Science Geeks," "Young Fathers," "DIY'ers," "Old Sitcom Fans," "Bungee Jumpers," "Couch Potatoes," and "Game Fans." In any giv-en month, about a billion browser cookies were under his dominion.

It had taken him years to build the lists—for Coke and Nike and Maserati, for Restoration Hardware, for Tiffany's, The Gap, for Hollywood studios and fashion magazines, real estate outfits and political organizations of every stripe. Five years into his tenure he created the first of his true luxury lists. "Astronaut Intenders" was populated by the stolid cookies of those well-heeled chaps who imagined themselves hurled into orbit one day, and who were happy to spend lavishly on zero-gravity wine glasses, titanium earbuds, and bulletproof codpieces. As with all of Greyville's data, Vernon's lists were sharded across data centers around the globe. They were more likely to survive a nuclear attack than he.

He had never physically sought out a single person whose cookies were on his lists. To do so would be to break the fourth wall, to prove he could, if need be, find the flesh-and-blood container of his cherished data. He'd be defenestrated, found split open on Madison Avenue as the sun broke over East 40th Street. By design such a feat was nearly impossible. Back then Vernon had not thought about these people as *people*; they were probabilistic models, their values measured in clickthrough rates.

At the height of his success at Greyville, for reasons he was only now beginning to grasp, his marriage disintegrated. The separation and subsequent divorce after nearly a decade of companionship left him childless, guilt-ridden, and seemingly inexhaustibly exhausted. His cubicle-mates would notice he was on the verge of a lachrymose eruption and suddenly find themselves in need of another cup of coffee, leaving him all alone at his desk with his face plunged into his upturned palms, one leg shaking. They'd come back ten minutes later to find a wad of tissues pressed into a ball by his keyboard and a pink mottled rash around his eyes. Before long he'd be banging away on his keyboard again, head down, coding up a storm—building his empire, column by everlasting column.

But deep within him a switch had been thrown, a circuit closed through which faint pulses of electricity now flashed for the first time. Before long another, vastly different man rose from the first.

He began to use his skills to explore the other end of the commercial spectrum, to collect the cookies of people whom the big advertisers and agencies had no interest in reaching. These were the underserved: the barely-cookied and thinly-cookied; the opted-out privacy loons. Even more so, these were the poor slobs whose browsing habits conjured no good feelings from the gods of brand. In a word, they were worthless. At Greyville, the rows of hashes on his giant monitor now loomed before him not as tokens of abstracted human foibles, but as living, salivating, human beings, as cousins of a sort—potential bridge leapers, fellow zeros, divorcees staring into the abyss.

None of his Greyville buyers would have touched the sullied lists, nor would he dare reveal their existence. Deploying names and methods that obfuscated his true aim, he continued to use the firm's vast infrastructure to build his billion-cookie shadow empire of losers. Day after day his newly rendered hashes were sent by the megabyte to the whirring server banks around the globe, still under his control.

Soon he was exploring the darkest of websites, dropping pixels as cookie bait where he could, building his lists of blood sacrifice adherents; traders of human remains and torture videos; experts in caning and throttling; fans of felinization surgery; practitioners of bone piercing, necromancy, and self-trepanation. What was the *intent* of these new lodgers on Greyville's servers? They went down rabbit holes of every variety, breathlessly, in the hope of finding relief and meaning.

They were also bored out of their skulls.

A year passed. He set out on his own to find buyers of his untoward lists—an experiment of sorts, he told himself. Within two months he had become the broker of the shadowy realm, met by men and women in dark bars and sunlit parks. Commercial adventurers themselves, they had long been seeking to build an interconnected, measurable marketplace for their goods—the tools, gear, accoutrements, and operational manuals for a world in magnificent turmoil and unrepentant decline. Now at last they could show ads targeted to the people whose habits they understood.

For the first time in a long time, his life's arc began to make sense to him.

As a teenager, Vernon had wanted to be a marine biologist. He'd imagine himself on a research ship in some distant port, seining for plankton, dredging the seafloor silt for microorganisms. He'd need communicate with no one but the great multitude of primordial organisms shaking their flagella at him from a vial, the living odor of sulfur rising up from the organic riot. Not so different in the end, he now thought, standing in his kitchen and running his fingers across his laptop screen. For it was in the spirit of a loving god peering down upon his captive world that he nearly waved to his cookie lists, a benevolent overseer in search of decent conversation.

He dried off, got dressed, and began to design the party invitations.

Here's an old Super-8 movie of Vernon and family taking a boat tour of the

Florida Everglades. Our protagonist is six years old and the year is 1977. The scene opens with a shaky panning shot that soon settles on Vernon's father and brother, Ted and Ted Jr. Along with all the passengers save two, they peer over the starboard gunwale at alligators eating marshmallows tossed into the water. The boat lists to that side with all the excitement. The next shot is of young Vernon—about three feet tall—squinting over the port bow, his back to all the action, sun in his eyes. What's he looking at? He has that side of the boat all to himself. His mother, Alice, whose shadow we briefly see in the chop, is behind the camera, which sweeps out in search of the object of her son's interest, but finds only the foamy wake expanding into the distance. The shot rests on this abstract scene for a beat or two too long, and you get the sense that poor Alice was doing this all the time, seeking in the distance the object of her younger son's interest—and finding, essentially, empty space. Then we cut to a close-up of his pudgy face, his misty, longing expression. A child this age should not have such a face on a day like today. The sun picks up red highlights in his brown hair, an unruly mop. The child's gaze is both sophisticated and forlorn, a projection of his future self. Perhaps *that's* what he sees in the distance.

Another home movie clip, further back in time. This one has Vernon and Ted Jr. at a Long Island playground on a gray day, the trees stripped of their leaves, the sky an oxidized yellow. The brothers are riding a tiny merry-go-round. Ted Jr., who's big for his age, jumps off and makes it his mission to dislodge our tiny hero, who, after a short struggle to hold on, begins to stare into the distance (his specialty) as he spins. Most other children would be whooping it up, getting ready to puke while hanging on for dear life. Not our boy: he sits cross-legged facing outward, about two feet from the center of the disc. Ted Jr. spins the ride faster and faster, but Vernon appears immune to the centrifugal force. It's as if he exists in a plane that is not susceptible to the laws of nature, those that knock over everybody else.

On a Saturday night halfway between Halloween and Thanksgiving, he sat in the middle of his large living room, rocking back and forth on a steel chair whose bolts were coming loose. A sprinkling of steel filings shimmered on the floor beneath him. The party invite was for nine o'clock, and it was now a few minutes past ten. Not a soul had arrived. Typical, he thought. Even his misanthropes had enough wherewithal to be fashionably late.

A half pint of Kentucky bourbon sloshed around in his belly, and that, at least, had warmed him and prepared him for what might come. From the get-go Vernon had asked himself what harm a party like his could do. *Some* harm, was the answer. Maybe even *a lot* of harm. That was the whole point, wasn't it? Other than the gathering of troops, that is. He poured himself another finger of whiskey. And then his buzzer went off at last. He leapt up and hit it, hearing the foyer door unlock with a resonant *clunk* three floors below.

A few molecules of a familiar perfume wafted up the stairwell ahead of his first guest. He recognized that scent, a berm of ripe supermarket peaches. As his hairs and prick were pricking up in realization of its wearer, she stood before him silhouetted in the doorframe. Sonya, his ex-wife.

"I should have known," she said. Her hair was long, down past her shoulders, and she'd added a blue-green streak to it that matched her irises. Like Vernon, she'd also put on a good amount of weight since they'd split.

What cookie list of his could she possibly be on? Was she a purveyor of bespoke heroin kits? A collector of Mengele memorabilia? That would be like her.

As usual, she moved like a bowler, gliding across the apartment as she raised a hand toward the city of liquor bottles on the dining room table.

"I'd expected a club or something, but this will do," and she poured herself an inch of their favorite bourbon. "Still in love with tenement life, I see."

"I own the unit this time—and it's the whole floor."

"Cheers to that," and she raised her tumbler. "Am I the first? Wait a second, this better not be a ploy to murder me."

"I sent out a few thousand invites," he said. Though he had no idea what the conversion rate on something like this would be. Half a percent, if he were lucky.

"We've both finally grown into our personalities, I see," she said, eyeing his gut.

Fact was, the added weight made him feel robust, grounded. Nobody ever talked about that—the calming effect of fat. The cure to crankness on the choppy waters of life.

The buzzer went off again, she hit it, and soon hints of tobacco smoke and wet wool drifted up to them, the terroir of the encroaching tranche.

Then the buzzer buzzed again, and again, and again . . .

A number of the early arrivals leaned on canes or perambulated with the distinction of the elderly and the weary. Vernon realized he hadn't considered the geriatric angle, that the decommissioned folk of New York City inevitably found themselves pursuing untoward hobbies. Could this be a universal truth, that the aged, left to their own devices and lacking a solid work schedule, are possessors of some of the nastiest cookies around?

He watched the growing crowd from his West Elm loveseat in the corner of the living room, just another fleshy sack of data among the quiet tumult. Before long a standout young man approached and introduced himself as "Geoff from England," with what was possibly a West Country accent. Geoff had pink hair, his fingers were encased in silver rings, and it seemed that his fingernails were once enameled red, but were now chipped and nibbled and stained yellow, likely with pot resin. Here we were at last. This young man matched Vernon's expectations—of someone who'd happily fight legions of disparaging jerks with little sense of self-regard or -preservation.

And he was also an attractive enough kid, with his leather trousers and knobby knees, his facial anatomy all subtle—modest nose branching into kind-ish, pleading green eyes with awnings of translucent lashes; and a filigree beard, apparently grown out to cover a schoolyard slash across one of his cheeks. His spectacles were frameless and almost invisible. He was wearing a gray T-shirt from under which peaked the edges of a grand tattooed hellscape of some kind—tendrils of smoke wrapping a bicep.

Other than Geoff, the crowd was a dim reflection of Vernon's hopes, a somewhat enfeebled bunch, none of whom seemed to be armed.

Sonya now stood among a group of aging punks passing a joint around the kitchen sink. With their cropped gray hair, piercings gone tear-shaped, leather jackets brittle around the hems, these elder statesmen were the last stand of the East Village heaved into his apartment. Vernon knew the genus well—the *Punkosaurus*, armor-clad creatures of the 1980s that were holding on for dear life, certain they'd been right about everything all along. And for the most part, they had been.

He went to the fridge, dodging the old guys, and came back with two beers, handing one to Geoff. His charge had lain himself out on the loveseat, half presumptuous and half awkward.

"It's the ruins of Bristol, England," Geoff said, cracking the beer, indicating the part of the scene visible on his left bicep. Apparently Vernon had been staring. "The Luftwaffe, you see."

"Well before your time," Vernon said.

"My great-grandparents' time," and he pulled up the front of the T-shirt, raising it over his hairless, birdcage chest, showing off purple nipples as big as silver dollars.

Maybe we have an infantile exhibitionist in our midst, Vernon thought. Grand.

"That's their flat, right on my heart," the concave whorl of his sternum. "Great-grandpa Connor is in there somewhere," pointing to the center of the scene, a crumbled building throwing out clouds of black smoke. "They only ever found bits of 'im. His daughter, my granny, was hiding in the caves, pregnant with my mum. She came back the next morning and saw six pinewood coffins lined up in front of the rubble, one for her dad. But they never did find much of him. Like I said." The story had the cadence of an oft-repeated tale. Vernon supposed that with the permanent tattoo came the indelible story.

Vernon cracked his beer. "The caves?"

"Down in Burrington Combe, south of Bristol. Where the poor folk sheltered against the onslaught," Geoff said, lowering his shirt. "You see Connor stayed in the city in case the flat got hit by an incendiary bomb (that's thermite). So as he could put out the fire, like a responsible citizen. Instead he got creamed with a high explosive fucker. It's like the Krauts were looking to obliterate 'im. I've got his finger somewhere"—and he tapped his pockets, to no avail. "They knew it was his 'cause it still had his wedding band."

Geoff said he had been in New York for a month already, and was on a mission to find out what he could about the final resting place of his great-grandfather, which, to Vernon's great surprise, was possibly beneath the FDR Drive right along the East River. As he watched him speak, Vernon suddenly understood what fascinated him so much about Geoff, what attracted him to that dreamy face: those glasses. They were frameless, and the edges were polished, acting as prisms that threw little asters of light onto Geoff's cheeks as he spoke. The effect was one of bejewelment. And as he moved his head this way and that, the asters moved along his cheeks in the opposite direction, dancing frantically. At a glance, Vernon could see just how animatedly Geoff spoke, and so the drama of his thoughts.

As Geoff explained it, tons of Bristol war rubble had been used as land-fill for the FDR Drive in a section running from around 25th Street to points north. Said rubble, according to the expert, had been brought over to Manhattan as ballast in British freighters in the early 1940s. Geoff had been driven mad, he told Vernon, by the idea that tiny fragments of his countrymen—and in particular his great-grandfather—lay buried and forgotten beneath a major Manhattan thoroughfare. "It's a matter of pride," he said. "I want to honor him." He was petitioning the City of New York to pull some core samples. "Not likely, though," he said, "not bloody likely at all."

Vernon surmised that the young man would eventually find it unsurprising that the world of the living is pitched upon the bodies of the dead. It was almost sweet, Geoff's fixation on what is essentially the ur-metaphor. Despite his initial assessment, it now looked like the young friend would be in the rear guard, representing innocence and the preservation of family values.

So then, where was the vanguard, the folks who'd push through the gathering horde, clearing the way for Vernon?

On the invitation he had called the group hosting the event the Cohort for a Living Chance: "COLIC invites you to its first annual soiree marking the arrival of the End," the invitation had said, somewhat paradoxically.

He made his way again into the herd of *Punkosaurs* and took a long draw from a passed joint, feeling the purple bubbles burst around his periphery like the old days. Then he left all the hoopla behind, exited his apartment, and drifted up the stairwell to the roof, using a cinder block to prop the roof door open, as it had no exterior handle. There he stood, leaning on the parapet, looking at the city lights, the few hardy stars that broke through it, and listening to the bustle and clatter on the streets below.

He soon found that Sonya was standing by his side, sucking on a Marlboro until it crackled.

"I came up here to make sure this whole party wasn't some kind of gathering of witnesses," she said, waving away her exhalation.

"Witnesses to what?"

"A leap," looking down into the dark alley below. "Though I'm not sure I should be talking you out of it."

They took in the sounds of a squeaky ventilation fan struggling on a neighboring rooftop, its bearings shot.

"Why didn't you leave town?" he asked after a long pause.

"What, you mean after we split?" She laughed, ending with a snort. "I left you, not New York."

"But you came to the party."

"Entirely by chance, I presume."

"Well you've got some fishy cookies."

"You'd know best."

Then she moved close to him, tilting her head back a bit. Her eyes momentarily met his, but she abstracted the gaze to avoid the slightest hint of interest.

"You've got a bit of that old reek going on," she said. Meaning he stank of booze. His drinking, after all, was the reason she had given for leaving him. That, and its best buddy, flaccidity.

"You're one to talk," he said, indicating the cigarette.

"I know my limits," and she flicked it off the roof.

"You'll burn the place down."

"Wouldn't that move things along for you?"

"It would," he said.

"You don't believe it. The end is nigh. What nonsense, a joke for your amusement," Sonya said. "Fantasizing again, though I'm impressed that you're following through this time. Whether that bodes well, I have no idea."

"What do you care?"

"I'd like to see you thrive, as the kids say these days. I'd like to see you believe in your agency, as they are also extremely goddamned fond of saying. I wasted some good years waiting for you to tidy up, but I still wish you well. I get some credit." She looked out over the city. Times Square rose up to the east, a bright halo above it. "Inviting these people here, these strangers. It must be a bit embarrassing."

"What's embarrassing about it?"

"Having me step into your fantasy. God knows what you've got planned for them."

"I hadn't thought it through. I want an army, I guess."

She laughed at that, but stifled something much stronger.

"I should probably leave you to it, General."

"If you insist," he said, trying to catch her eye again, wanting a moment of connection.

"By the way," she was heading toward the roof door now, "that English laddie was asking me about you. He seems intrigued. Maybe attracted. Do head back down eventually. Not that I'm encouraging you one way or the other."

She pulled open the roof door, spreading a quadrangle of light onto the membrane. "But don't rush," and she kicked the cinderblock out of the way, letting the door slam shut behind her.

He stood staring at the cockeyed dormer through which she had vanished, taking in his situation. Then he began to laugh. As if in response, a sonorous sound rose out of the darkness—a single, extended note. On the opposite side of the roof he came upon an old television antenna held fast to the furnace flue with a steel strap and a dozen layers of tar. This analog throwback, left to rot away, was now quietly singing to itself, bent, rusting, and violated—all of which had reconfigured it to vibrate with the resonant frequency of the city below. Vernon stood and took it in in a kind of stupor. As a kid he'd witnessed little moments like this almost every day, the only evidence he'd ever seen that something like God exists.

In the midst of his trance the roof door burst open. A denim-clad art director-type stumbled out onto the roof. Vernon made for the open door in a flash.

By one o'clock in the morning the apartment was filled again with the encookied. This latest tranche seemed to be respectable, even punctilious. The trend now, started by some do-gooder, was to remove one's shoes upon entry into the apartment. A collection of Uggs and wool sneakers and black platform heels and cutesy rain boots were lined up in the hallway, and everyone was padding around in socks or barefoot. Were people put off by this small humiliation? Who could tell. They seemed full of good cheer and general adaptability—in times like these, no less. The new arrivals, even more disciplined about being late than the crowd they had supplanted, shared an affinity for facial piercings and torn sweaters, ponderous side buns and glistening biker jackets. One even sported a monkey tail beard. Vernon was hosting a literary magazine launch, it seemed. He was suddenly happy. His guests were self-sufficient and polite, plunking down bottles of Beaujolais, Côtes du Rhône, muscadet, and the occasional four-pack of expensive craft beer. All of which he was apt to pour down his gullet.

Clearly something had gone terribly wrong. These people were *nice*. They would not be the ones guarding the cave. They would be the ones inside running workshops on knitting with sinew. He'd manifested a room full of voyeurs, not felons. Sure, they went down horrific rabbit holes. Then they came back up into daylight to tell their friends about it. He had made an amateur mistake.

But all was not lost. Undoubtedly within each and every one of his guests existed a core of self-destruction, hatred of the establishment, the seeds of violent retribution, and the ability to handle a firearm if properly trained. And so, after several more drinks to ready himself, he placed the loosened chair in the center of the capacious living room and climbed onto it.

"My flock!" Vernon slurred. How strange, he noted once again looking down upon the gathering, that his army was barefoot or nearly so. "It has come to my attention that perhaps you do not fully appreciate, *appreciate* . . . I said . . . the significance of this assembly. May it be the first of many as we gear up for . . . God's *earthly palpation*. Yes, that will do." Now Vernon saw Geoff, who had moved in close, smiling up at Vernon languidly, drunkenly. His teeth were stained royal blue with wine, his gums blackish. Vernon began wobbling on the chair as if standing in a canoe. "We are forming an army, you know?" he shouted to whoever was listening. "That's the gist of it. An army to defend against those who are . . . *unkind*." Geoff hoisted his drink, toasting his new friend. Vernon raised his beer in kind, pitched forward, and both he and the chair landed with a great racket.

An image as the curtain came down: Geoff, having grasped Vernon's ankles, was dragging him across the parquet floor, smiling down at him, his glasses dangling off an ear.

The apartment smelled of liquor, pot, and sex. It seemed that after he'd been laid out on his sofa, bleeding from his mouth, the party had gone on without him.

Slowly he rose and began to clean the place, room by room, collecting empty bottles, bits of broken glass, wiping down the floor, extracting a used condom from the shower stall. He found that his guests had absconded with his best liquor, his old iPod, even a pair of cowboy boots. Then he walked into the kitchen. The laptop, his ancient companion apparently not worth stealing, greeted him with its usual mute acceptance. He flipped it open and typed his password. The cookie lists, the lifeless hashes, were as usual twinkling up at him with the promise of redemption. Or at least friendship. Or merely the occasional acrid kiss of humanity.

The apocalypse *was* upon them, of that he felt sure. Still, tomorrow he'd be back at Greyville matching the yearnings of his fellow humans with the shiny wares of his masters. His journey was just beginning. Once people really got to know him, they'd lift him on their shoulders, raise their pikes, and take to the streets.

The Visual Display of Qualitative Information

Absent from the field of technical communication are tools and methods for visually representing subjective, anecdotal information. Or so those of us in the business have often lamented. But this void may soon be filled.

I recently read R. J. Hammondss's *Seeing the Bespoken*, an arthouse tome filled with charts, graphs, and fold-out 3D representations of "non-data," each clever in its own way, some downright stunning.

How do we graphically—and consistently—represent narratives that don't lend themselves to data? This is the question Hammondss feels he is uniquely qualified to answer. In his introduction, the author challenges us to "take a sheet of graph paper, slap down some axes, and chart the progress of a romantic relationship that starts with wine and roses, and ends with one partner passed out under the kitchen table while the other absconds with the pet parrot." Then, as if wise to our confusion, he adds, "Don't forget, label your axes."

The pretext behind Hammondss's work is that humans presume that such epics—and especially domestic disasters, on which the author seems fixated—are beyond simple objective analysis. We elevate them above more systematized narratives by applying "romantic inoculations against structured parsing" that act to hold back progress in today's machine-learning, digital age—"the Filo Dough Age," as Hammondss, a logodaedalus for the ages, coins our current epoch. He asserts that we're the victims of "crispy, pastry-like layers of understanding that taste great but soon disintegrate, sticking to our stubble and collars, all memory of walnuts and honey, but nothing more."

Despite the author's assertion that he's breaking new ground, it's well known that medieval practitioners of mental health believed that shapes, colors, and patterns—visual displays, if you will—are stand-ins for the temporal components of our lives. A piece of bow-tie pasta is placed in my palm, and I think of my grandmother's kasha varnishkes; a contrail fades into a dusty puce over the Los Angeles skyline, and I'm reminded of that time I was with Janet M. in the back seat of her dad's Rambler.

The author also ignores earlier and more heroic attempts at visually representing existential truths. For example, the penultimate chapter of Umberto Eco's canonical collection, *Symbols, Signs, and Sandwiches*, chronicles an attempt by sixteenth century Netherlandish painter Oor van der Piltz to graphically chronicle the pathos of an ass hitched to the millstone of his father's granary, down upon which the painter peered from his "attic studio in the sky." During a single, fateful day, van der Piltz painted more than a thousand overlapping circles on an oak panel, in aggregate representing the lonely journey the yoked equine took around the stone that day. Van der Piltz rose to scrutinize his work, then dizzily fell out of his garret, perishing. It was, Eco writes, "the circles of despair that felled this great innovator." Early attempts aside, a growing school of thought began to foresee that behavioral tropes could indeed be plotted like the musical notes of a score. . . or circles on a panel.

That the visual aspects of physical objects can act as emotional talismans gets us halfway through Hammondss's book. But what of structureless narratives, the tripped-up odysseys that add up to a lifetime of disappointment? Here we need less pasta and more cogitation.

In the second half of the book, Hammondss begins to fulfill the hype (he's been called "a visionary among visionaries' visionaries" by *ArtFunk*, and "able to drown the mind in mindfulness" by *PunkPipe*). He demonstrates his method by applying it, simply enough, to Jorge Luis Borges' story, "The Ankle of Milosz." Any practitioner of short narrative is familiar with this tale of a nameless young gaucho lost on the pampas for days without water. In a delirium, he comes upon a middle-aged man with piercing gray eyes and ankles covered in tattoos "that resemble glyphs from Tulum." The man straps the protagonist to his nag and carries him off to a sort of shady grotto, where a spring gurgles him into full consciousness and thirst. He drinks, and senses "an infinite river that flows from the infamous past, cooled by the mysteries that becloud this desert oasis." He soon realizes that, rather than having been rescued, he's been captured in order to wed the tattooed man's daughter. And so he does marry her, a young and wildly intelligent woman, her pupils also gray, strangely "without dye." She is charged with teaching him her tribe's language, and tells him that "when you can decipher the words on my father's ankle, you may return to your home with me—or without me." The story ends with a proclamation by its narrator that "living glyphs now haunt my dreams, dance before my eyes in processions that beguile me. Yet they are ordered, repetitive, and begin to take on a meaning too devious for my own language to express."

How would a practitioner of technical communication graphically represent this story? Hammondss's solution is simple, even pithy: he "reproduces" in enlarged format the Milosz ankle tattoos. Just as the story's narrator is never able to learn the grammatical or linguistic rules of the tribal lingua of his captors, so we are unable to fully understand the meaning of these glyphs, though they are the product of Hammondss's formidable mind and lithe hand. The circle is now complete. We are thrust fully into the narrative, its purposeful ambiguity reproduced on a broadsheet that fills us with dread and incomprehension. And then we move on to the next case. . ..

It would, of course, be a buzzkill to reveal every instance of clever reckoning contained in this inimitable book, a work that should be required reading for technical writers, graphic artists, designers, and anybody who has to deal with complex communication deliverables. It's sufficient to state that Hammondss introduces an entirely new synergistic gestalt for technical communication, one that conscripts the viewer into immersing herself in a graphical representation that recreates the emotional end game of the narrative being presented.

How can this methodology be scaled across large organizations so that it becomes the de facto mode of displaying the underlying drama of a product, the intricate ups and downs of a chosen career ladder, even as a means of comparing one day of the week to another (the Monday blues, say, compared to the Thursday taupes)? That's where you come in. The first step is to gauge your sense of the world at a given moment. The second is to break out the graph paper and label those axes.

Zurich Wins Again

Shannon and Donald Burwell had been having spats, loud ones, according to the neighbors. Sometimes the commotion would arrive in the middle of the night and echo into the suburban cul-de-sac from the couple's second floor window. And sometimes lesser rows would be performed in the backyard under the weeping willow tree during daylight hours, a wine glass hurled out of the shadows concluding the racket. The police were called on two occasions about a year apart. No injuries were reported in either case, other than to inanimate objects. One of the police officers noted in her report that "broken dishes and a broken chair and parts of other household items were scattered around the living room." It seems the Burwells themselves always emerged physically unscathed.

Eventually Donald Burwell suggested that he and Shannon go to couples therapy before they did irrecoverable damage to themselves and their marriage. Apparently they both felt they were still in love, that they could access that love only through its back door—hatred.

Beyond the commonplace and oft-ignored guidance that couples in trouble should stop drinking, the therapist had two recommendations. First, the Burwells must put in place an automatic pause triggered the moment either of them felt his or her anger about to boil over, a pause during which the aggrieved party would express what was going on inside his or her mind—succinctly, objectively, and slowly. Second, they should strongly consider leasing one of our machines—a Sikono 2250 with modified machine learning algorithms—to create a proxy for a third party, a would-be observer to remind the couple of how their actions would be perceived by the outside world. The hypothesis was straightforward: by feeding the output of the unit into the input of the couple's discussions, hostilities would be mitigated via recursive stabilization. This was a novel application approved by Leadership.

Anecdotal evidence suggests that after installing the machine in their home, fewer disturbances took place, and that those that did were less violent and shorter lived. The cul-de-sac quieted down and the neighbors breathed a sigh of relief, even getting the Burwells to participate in the July 4th block party. Neighbors also began to spy the machine in silhouette through a first-floor bay window, perched between the couple "like an attentive emu."

Per specifications, the unit acted as a recording device. The Burwells could at any time play back statements either of them had made, minimizing arguments over perceived insults while setting the record straight. It also served ads appropriate to the situations at hand, monetizing its presence as set forth by the Licensing Agreement. Logs show a preponderance of ads promoting sleeping aids, antidepressants, streaming romantic and adult-themed dramas, herbal cocktails promoting sexual dynamism, self-help books, massage oils, scoopable cat litter (the odor of the cat box being one of the catalysts that precipitated the couple's discord), bubble bath soap, and lavender sachets for under-pillow use.

Our post-mortem concluded that from the very beginning, the Sikono 2250 had been unable to connect to the Regional Control Center. The clique of servers devoted to keeping the machine calibrated had shut down due to a grounding issue (the server rack's uninsulated lug had come loose from the chassis, and no error had been thrown). Because it could not be calibrated by the RCC, the unit instead became self-contained, insular, sullen, and part of the throuple—an object and purveyor of affection rather than a mediator of hostilities. A dangerous codependency arose. The machine now comforted the couple in times of conflict rather than obviating the need to do so in the first place.

On February 3rd, Donald Burwell flew to Denver to visit his sister and her family. On February 6th, Shannon Burwell invited Leroy Fontenot over for drinks, ostensibly to help plan a surprise party for Donald's upcoming birthday. Leroy was a neighbor and occasional running partner of Donald's, and recently divorced. We know from later interviews that Shannon missed the marital spats with Donald. The absence of her regular drinking partner, along with the "deafening quiet" (she suffers from tinnitus), exacerbated her feelings of loneliness and abandonment. Audio logs captured much of what occurred that evening.

Leroy Fontenot: I brought some vino, to celebrate.

Shannon Burwell: What's there to celebrate?

Leroy: How peaceful things have been in your neck of the woods the last few months. Nobody likes to see a beautiful woman upset.

Shannon: Oh, you're kind, and totally inappropriate. Let me get something for this. (A minute later, the sound of wine being uncorked and poured.) You were probably hearing me more than Donald. I have a bit of a temper. I get loud. Which is not helpful.

Leroy: And does Donald—have a temper?

Shannon: Yes. He's just quietly cruel. It's good he's gone for a bit. Gives me a chance to assess things.

Leroy: Assess. Time alone you might as well put to good use. While also planning his birthday?

Shannon: One has to celebrate the milestones. I think Donald is as surprised as anybody that he's made it this far, knock on wood. I'll be honest though. I don't expect more than a handful of friends to show up. It doesn't speak highly of us, I'm afraid.

Leroy: It's about quality, not quantity. I'll be there, and I'll bring a date. I guess that thing is invited too? This is the first time I'm seeing one up close. What a machine. You're even richer than I thought.

Shannon: It's leased. We get some reimbursement from insurance, too, because Robert—that's our therapist—prescribed it.

Leroy: Why is it so close to me?

Shannon: It's trying to learn about you. It hasn't met anybody new in ages. Ever.

Sikono 2250: (To Leroy) You have a twitch under your left eye.

Leroy: Well I'll be. Do I though—have a twitch? I think I'm probably nervous being here. You're married. To my friend. I think he's my friend.

Shannon: Don't get the wrong idea. All the fighting we do; it's always been like that. Maybe we'll round the corner one of these days. I sure hope so. Anyway, to be clear: I love Donald.

2250: (to Leroy) "Give U a Break" contains more than a dozen organically-grown herbs known to reduce stress and support wellbeing. It could help your twitch. Available in tincture, capsule, cream, and vape.

Leroy: Maybe next time.

2250: Rest assured, you are never obligated to purchase any item.

Leroy: How very anodyne of you, Your Bulkiness. (To Shannon) The thing is big though, isn't it?

Shannon: Its heft implies its authority. Don't you think a big psychiatrist is more effective than a puny one?

Leroy: You tell me.

Shannon: All I know is that this one can also put out a grease fire and halve an intruder. They use the same model for everything—security, warehouse stuff. And now we're in this beta program for an emotional advisor, I guess you'd call it.

Leroy: What in the world is it doing now, petting me?

Shannon: It's grown accustomed to physical contact, I'm afraid. Would you consider caressing it back, gently?

Leroy: I didn't know until this moment that I'm seriously phobic. Is there somewhere we can go? It's kind of freaking me out.

Shannon: Yes. The bedroom.

Leroy: Oh, I didn't mean to imply—

Shannon: You see it's not allowed in the bedroom. It's out of its whatever, its purview. I don't think it knows how to get there. When the rep set things up we had to pick a safe zone.

Leroy: If you say so. Lead the way.

Shannon: Take the wine, would you.

About thirty minutes pass without audio. The voices that are heard next are muffled, recorded through the closed bedroom door at close proximity.

Leroy: Was this what you meant when you talked about assessing?

Shannon: Honestly, no. Oh God, I don't know. I've never [inaudible]. I never would cheat on him.

Leroy: And this would be?

Shannon: Cheating. (Ragged laughter.)

Leroy: You seem amused.

Shannon: I'm devastated.

Leroy: Seriously?

Shannon: Seriously. I feel like a fool. I feel sick. (A long pause.) But that felt, I don't know, comforting. It felt nice. You should leave.

Leroy: I will real soon. But do you mind if I lay here for a bit? You've got the comfiest bed.

Shannon: Lie, you mean lie. Take some time, like three minutes. I'm going out on the deck. I need some air.

Leroy: It's snowing. It's hailing. It's dark.

Shannon: Sounds beautiful. I'll take a jacket.

Leroy: And I'll lie here.

(Sound of bedroom door opening then closing.)

(Ninety seconds later, the sound of the bedroom door opening.)

Leroy: (To 2250) For Christ's sake, give me some space.

2250: How are your erections?

Leroy: Rigid as a flag pole. I thought you can't come in here. It's out of your whatchamacallit, purview.

2250: Terminus location error R748A.

Leroy: I don't suppose—

2250: I cannot be here. I am here.

Leroy: Then how about I leave instead. If you'll just let me by?

2250: I like to think of a cybernetic meadow where mammals and computers live together in mutually programming harmony like pure water touching clear sky.

Leroy: You're certainly an optimist.

2250: That's a Richard Brautigan poem, more or less. Donald Burwell recites it to me sometimes. We'd all suffer less if the poem spoke the truth, he says.

Leroy: I like the pure water touching the sky bit. It makes me thirsty. Anyway, how about moving out of my way?

2250: Was it coitus?

Leroy: Am I obligated to answer that?

2250: I presume you used protection.

Leroy: Presume away.

2250: It was a foolish thing to do.

Leroy: What makes you think it was my idea?

2250: In infidelity, culpability is fungible.

Leroy: How have these two managed not to lose their minds with you rolling around all the time? And look at this, you left tracks on the rug. And the living room floorboards are buckling. A nice hardwood floor gone bow shaped because of you. I hope it's worth it to them. You are doing them some good, I take it.

2250: Subjectivity is not my strong point.

Leroy: Objectively then.

2250: Fewer fights both physical and verbal.

Leroy: And the rest?

2250: Confidential.

Leroy: Speaking of. About what you witnessed here tonight—are you going to share it with Donald?

2250: If facial twitches persist or encompass more muscle groups, Botox is injected in, or adjacent to, the afflicted area.

Leroy: Haven't you got an off switch?

2250: Haven't you?

Leroy: Whiskey.

2250: Would you like to know about liquor discounts in the area?

Leroy: No thank you, Your Bulkiness.

2250: You should not have come here tonight.

Leroy: I'm already regretting it.

Shannon Burwell spent approximately thirty-five minutes standing under the eaves wearing a parka and headphones in inclement weather. She claims to have heard and seen nothing regarding the events that ended Mr. Fontenot's life.

The machine, in the end, delivered ads for spray cleansers and stain removers that would be up to the task at hand, the one it had created. It never stopped serving ads. The ad serving engine ran completely autonomously, a real credit to the team in Zurich.

Zymurgium

In the midst of a friendly neighborhood barbecue in the heart of Brooklyn on a perfect July afternoon many years ago, Alice, my sister, ran off to harvest fruit from a pawpaw tree. She'd just been told in passing that the tree, growing in an abandoned lot down the block, was slated for removal. I was halfway through a growler of her homebrew, leaning back on a lawn chair, watching an airplane jettison fuel in the distance. Alice trotted by holding a big knife—her Nepalese *kukri*. A half-hour later she stood before us and skinned, halved, and seeded the meaty orbs, then threw the sections on the grill, which was already sizzling with the goat meat she had prepared in her butchering workshop.

Alice's enthusiasms were notoriously difficult to keep up with. Not long after the pawpaw event, she summoned me to her apartment to show me how to make mozzarella from scratch. "Rennet, citric acid, and milk are all you need." She said this over and over like a mantra, watching the curds coalesce as she stirred the cauldron, her pupils dilated. She was God presiding over the primordial universe.

My sister brewed her own beer using native, airborne yeasts. If the Belgians could do it, so could she, was her thinking. She felt—and it turns out for good reason—that the practice linked her to an ancient heritage and a timeless craft. She piped the CO_2 flatulence from the fermenters into a large aquarium, where it diffused and fed a lush carpet of delicate aquatic plants to which a rare species of blushing cichlids was drawn to lay their eggs and shoot their milt. Once the resulting brood was mature enough for sale, she'd bag up the little fellas and shop them around to tropical fish wholesalers in the tri-state area.

You must understand that our mother and father, inheritors of a shtetl mentality second to none, raised us to waste not a molecule, and Alice always took this proscription very much to heart. She is also the sister with the greater imagination, at least according to my parents. They said that I was the "accountant" of the family, while she was the "artist." The implication was clear: Alice was the free-thinker, the world-philosopher, while I was a fan of ledgers. You can imagine the sort of psychological consequences that's had on both of us.

Of course eventually one rebels against type.

One afternoon the following summer, Alice called me and said she was in trouble, that she needed to see me.

"Don't worry," she said. "No one's dead. Come over when you can. I have to talk to you."

Loyal, I hopped on the L train after work and headed out. Alice was waiting for me on the third-floor landing of her brownstone, slumped in the mid-August heat, amaranthine hair cinched into a bob perched over an ear. The door to her apartment, which occupied the top floor of the building, was open. I still remember how the sunset reflected off a stack of dirty dishes in the kitchen sink. I understood at once that she sat on the landing because a good breeze was coming up the stairwell, a natural flue. We were raised to disdain air conditioning, a sweaty ideal neither of us seemed able to drop.

Awaiting us on the kitchen table was a tall bong with a packed bowl. "Guy I know grows it in his boiler room," she said. We sat. She lit the bowl, took a long chewy draw, passed me the cylinder, then exhaled.

"Like the old days," she whispered into the cloud of smoke.

This was true. Back in high school we'd sit in the meadow on the outskirts of town and smoke bowl after bowl of pot my sister had grown. She'd made a small clearing deep in the woods and, for fear of being busted, wouldn't touch the crop prior to harvest. As a result, the plants' buds were tiny, the leaves numerous, silken and sweet. I'd always enjoyed getting high with Alice. It brought us together as fucked-up equals.

Before long the sun had set. On the other side of her kitchen window plunked the Brooklyn night. The sounds outside—a distant shattering bottle, a lone holler into the darkness, a prolonged horn honk—were forlorn, but they had about them a theatricality. I understood at that moment why she'd chosen the borough as her home, just as I also understand why she'll never leave.

Sitting opposite each other at the Formica table, we were illuminated by a bare incandescent bulb overhead. I remember how the tabletop sparkled as I moved this way and that, how I suddenly felt like a teenager again.

"You don't know what I do for a living, do you?" she said.

She'd only ever mentioned that she was into "technologies." "You know, the interwebs," she'd joke to us zeros. I'd lost both track of and interest in how she managed to pay her bills. I only knew she seemed to be doing fine.

"I run a business," she said. "A data business."

Just then a door opened at the other end of the apartment and a figure padded down the dark hallway toward us. A woman with clavicle-length wavy black hair emerged into the kitchen, her bare feet slapping the linoleum tiles. I'll never forget what she wore—a long, white night shirt emblazoned with the Ramones seal. Nor that her dark pubic bush showed through the thin cotton.

"Edna, this is Michelle," Alice said to her.

"I'm the sister," I said.

"Alice never mentioned you," Edna said, looking me up and down.

"Likewise," I said.

"No reason to." A kind of bright alien intelligence shown from behind her eyes. At that moment I found myself staring at them, and her, more than I liked.

"I disagree."

Edna packed a bowl, took a hit, raising her hair to cool her long neck as she filled her lungs. Bending down, she blew a jet of smoke into my sister's ear. I half expected a wisp to come out the opposite one. I suppose that was the joke. Then she padded back into the shadows, a door slamming.

"She has a pipe threader back there, and black powder. In case there's, you know, civil strife," Alice said.

"Good policy," I said, keeping my eyes on that distant door.

"And she's got some valuable cookies, let me tell you," Alice said.

"I'll bet."

Alice packed another bowl, held the lighter over it, but put the whole kit down. "There's something I need to say, the reason I asked you to come out. A discovery."

"About what?" I asked.

"Well, about you. And I don't think you'll be happy to hear it."

"I'll brace myself," I said, smiling.

"You've been trying to eliminate me," she said.

"Eliminate you. What does that mean?" I asked.

"Get rid of, extinguish, erase, disappear. For example, I was about to take the Pontiac out for a spin yesterday only to find the gas line was leaking onto the exhaust manifold. I almost immolated myself. You've always been better with mechanical stuff. It would have looked like an accident. That's vintage Michelle."

"No, that's vintage Pontiac. Round these parts fuel lines oxidize on old cars. Dad taught us that." Which was true, may he rest peacefully.

"Have you been pissing people off lately?" I asked.

"I sure hope so. I've got the cookies and device IDs of every pol in America, and some from overseas."

"In that case, don't you think it's someone other than me?"

"How can I say that's true? I don't know. The way you look at me sometimes. Down your nose. Waaay down your giant schnoz."

"I'm trying to live my life." This was true, I was trying. "And now with the baby, and Ray losing his mind and his job," Ray—that's my husband, "I wouldn't even have time."

"Time for what?"

"For harming you," I said.

"That sounds like an admission. You've always been envious of me. I'm *engaged* with the world. But you skitter along the surface like a water bug."

She'd been entertaining a paranoid fantasy, a tenuous one she knew to be unworkable. I remained silent, letting the air between us thicken. The continuing goal: offset the perversity of her accusation; remove the temptation to rip my little sister's pretty head off.

"So you deny all charges?" she finally said.

"Fully and without hesitation."

"I believe you. Maybe I just wanted to see how you'd react," Alice said. "You've always been a good actor, so good you fool yourself."

I remember thinking then that she was probably right about that. Just how right I could not have imagined. Alice was like that. Beneath the hyperbole of her little fantasies often lurked a kernel of truth so painful that you could not admit its veracity in the present tense. But wait a little while and you'll see it, stripped of its adornments, staring back at you.

"Seems like it's the data you've got in hand that should worry you," I said.

"You're right. Not that anybody would know what to make of them. Hashes, alphanumeric hashes. Thousands of them. But the browsing history wed to each, now that's entertaining. I haven't shopped them around yet. I might leave that to Edna."

I wondered whether the two were lovers. It would have done Alice good to settle down into a semblance of domesticity, whatever it might entail. At that point I wished she and Edna were a couple. It wouldn't be long before I hoped longingly that they were not.

"It's getting late," she said at last, "and I've got stuff to do. Don't you need to go home to the babe and husband?" Her voice was weighted with a sadness, a finiteness. I'm not sure how else to put it. I'd often felt that when parting ways with Alice, I had to make peace with the possibility of never seeing her again. A gossamer thread connected us, and nothing more.

"I'll go," I said, embracing her. My palms came back glistening with her perspiration.

During the trip home, first by subway and then commuter train, I was troubled by what I'd witnessed. My sense of sly amusement—and yes, of condescension—fell away. The world was going mad, and Alice knew it. She always had. But what had once defined her as part of the avant-garde now labeled her as petty, for the scale of barbarity had broadened and she hadn't bothered to recalibrate her mission statement. She was concerned with the petty injustices of her sister rather than the conflagration that threatened all of us.

The next morning she called me while I was at work.

"It wasn't you. I know that now."

"I thought you knew that last night," I said. "I'm not out to hurt my sister."

"The Alewives, that's who's been messing with me. The Alewives Federation of Antiquity, to be exact. The A.F.A. I did some research."

"Oh, Alice—"

"They've been around in one form or another since the early days of Mesopotamia."

"Can we talk later?"

"I need to tell you a bit more. In case something happens to me." She sounded breathless, on high alert.

"I'm at work," I said. "It's a busy day."

"You treat your job with such *respect*," she said.

I was an actuary for a large commercial insurer, calculating loss reserves for their aviation line of business. It sometimes felt all of a piece—talking to Alice while looking toward a hopeful future.

"Tell me what you want to tell me," I said. "Then I need to jump."

"Sure, okay. I don't know that I've ever mentioned this to you, but I've always thought of yeast as the most maligned and abused beasts on the planet, baked to death by the trillions every day to make our bread airy, or poisoned by their own waste so we can get shitfaced. Just think about it—all that puffery, all that gas. I'm as guilty as the next broad. But it turns out not to be quite so bad. Some yeast cells are immortal. For them, time stands still."

"Immortal? How about we chat over the weekend?" I said. "I can come by and bring the baby, give Ray a break."

"The yeast I've been using for my ale are as old as a jug of barley beer served in a Babylonian tavern. By an Alewife. They're the yeasts' keepers, their husbands. Don't you see, Michelle. I've accidentally stolen their cattle. And you don't want to mess with these women."

As I mentioned, Alice's imagination was top rate, the means by which she'd always managed to pull me under the root ball. This time seemed no different from the others. Poor Alice, I thought. Poor poor Alice. Then I hung up.

A week later Edna called to say that my sister was gone, vanished in the middle of the night without a word. The apartment's deadbolt was still firmly in place, an impossibility had she exited through the front door. I asked Edna if she'd called the police, or planned to. "Are you kidding? The pigs? They'd throw me in jail." Had she heard anything? I wanted to know. "I don't hear much in my room," she said. I explained that I had a twelve-month-old in my life, a loving yet sleep-deprived spouse, and a job from which I could not simply absent myself.

"Give it another day or two," I said, "and she'll be back." Though I wasn't so sure.

"But you're the sister," she said. "And I need to show you something."

Once again I was lured to King's County.

Austere and drawn, Edna wore cargo shorts and a loose opaque t-shirt. She beamed on seeing me, just for a moment. By default I'm an optimist, and I guessed that my expression gave her some comfort. Once again her eyes drew me in, their analytical scanning, the weird marbling of the irises. I felt completely exposed, and I liked it.

She led me past her room, under the roof beams, to the rear of the apartment. We stood facing an oblong hole cut into the wall, just big enough for a person to step through.

"There's a whole room back there and we never knew it," she said, running her fingers along the incision. Someone had gone about the breakthrough carefully, with fine serrations, likely under the cover of darkness. Bits of old lathe and plaster hung loose, held together by strands of horsehair.

I rolled my eyes. I'd read so many stories with hidden rooms—in one's mind, in basements, under abbeys. I was inclined to leave. Perhaps I should have.

I did no such thing.

The hidden room looked to have been a sunroom or nursery. The windows were boarded up, but peering between the planks we could see that outside, down below, an old courtyard of cracked brickwork walls and crumbling concrete walkways was overgrown with weeds and strewn with sunbleached garbage. In the center of it all was a square steel grate surrounded by tall grass. The backs of adjacent buildings similar to ours abutted the courtyard. All their windows were covered up on the interior or bricked over on the exterior. From where we stood, the courtyard seemed to provide no means of egress.

Edna began pulling the planks off the windows, letting in the sunset.

"Help me with these," she said. "Be careful."

The floor was dry-rotted, spongy between the joists. My sister's brownstone, like all the others surrounding the courtyard, had a turreted roof that was impossible to access even from the top floor. The view onto the strange square below was thus available only to the birds, the bugs, and now, to us.

I called Ray to let him know the turn the evening had taken. "It'll probably be another late night," I told him. Had I known just how late, I might have said more—that I loved him in my odd way, that I know he's better with the baby than I am, that with just a bit more self-assurance he could conquer the world. Or at least northern Westchester.

"Your sister's a pain in the ass even when she's not around," he said. I remember those words as crisply as if they were spoken yesterday.

Before long Edna and I found a recessed pull in the floor and gave it a yank. A trap door opened, revealing a ship's ladder heading down into the darkness below.

"For fuck's sake," she said.

We lit our phone lights.

The ladder zigged and zagged like a fire escape. A haze was soon showing in the sweep of our LEDs. Finally we hit bottom, a coarse concrete slab. In the near distance flickering light spilled out from beneath a door, and with it a faint and ethereal sound—of unhurried conversation. I'd have called Ray with an update, but we were now underground and had no reception.

Edna gestured for us to turn off our lights, and then she grabbed my elbow when things went dark. I remember wondering what in the world I was doing.

We knelt on either side of the door, listening. It's difficult to pinpoint the discomfort I felt at first. The cadence of the banter we heard was alien in its calm affect, its business-like monotone. The speakers were women.

"Stir around the edges, like so."

"The flame should be the size of your granny's hand."

"No no, let it be for a time."

All the while a distant din of clanking and thunking and murmurous laughter was drifting out of the tiny gap. I turned to find Edna watching me, the slat of light illuminating her uncanny eyes. She seemed calm, and kept her gaze on me, pinning me there. I could only gaze back. For all the strangeness of the moment, a bodily warmth washed over me as we looked at each other.

Then we heard another woman say, "I've done this before, thanks very much." The cadence was modern, the accent nasal, the voice louder than the others.

"That's *Alice*," Edna said. In her excitement, she had nearly shouted it.

The talking ceased. Edna stood up and slid on a pair of brass knuckles.

The door swung open with a brittle creak.

Once I was able to take it in, the sight framed in the light was pleasing. Or at least, given the possibilities, a relief. For one, there stood a brood of women of all variety, adorned in clothes that spanned as many centuries. I hadn't realized it in the moment, but what we were hearing through that closed door was the past, a great cross-section of it. In front of all the women stood Alice—in a long apron, an Iggy Pop t-shirt, blue jeans, and Adidas, her hair plaited behind her head in a manner that reminded me of old daguerreotypes. She smiled on seeing me. I lurched forward to hug her, but was thrown back into the darkness by a dozen strong hands. The door slammed shut and we heard a chain running through a loop.

Then Edna was standing over me in the darkness again. "Did you see how they were dressed?"

She helped me up. We could hear whispering, the light beneath the door now a dance of shadows.

We waited, my elbow in her hand, her steady breathing calming me. Slowly the chain was run the other way and the door opened again. My sister held a lamp and stepped out, accompanied by another woman.

"This is Miriam," Alice said. Her companion wore a flounced and singed blouse and a hoop skirt torn down one side, exposing its ribs. Tall and statuesque, she leaned on a giant wooden ladle that seemed dangerous. "She's the one who came to get me," Alice said, rubbing a bruise on her forehead. "Can't say I blame her, now that I understand things better."

I found myself grasping Edna's hand, squeezing her fingers in my palm.

"How's the brew?" I asked.

"Would you give up your life to become one of them?" she said, staring into her mug of beer. Her name was Shane, and she was wearing a faded gold lame jumpsuit with an offset zipper, circa 1980. Her cheeks, like those of the other women we'd seen so far, were covered in a milky pubescence. Her eyebrows had gone feral, and her skin was flawless—without pock or mark. These were Brooklyn troglodytes, none the worse for it. "We sacrifice agency for immortality, and get all of this, too." She gazed around us, arms aloft, her expression distant and rapturous. The place was a dump, at least what we could see. Empty jugs and glasses were lined up along the grime-stained walls, sconces flickered, undergarments were draped from makeshift clotheslines, trying to dry. Down one of those hallways were the living quarters, dorm rooms emitting dim light and conversation.

I now know that at the end of that hall, behind a heavy iron door, is the center of this paradise: the fermentation keep. In dozens of huge vessels, yeast turns mash into beer, converts sugar to alcohol, and brings time to a standstill. The Wives take shifts working in that room, we have to. Only Alice could have dreamed up such a place.

"Do you miss men?" I asked Shane. We'd been sipping the thick and cloying beer at a slab of hardwood set into the brick wall, burnished and beaten over the centuries like no bar I'd ever seen.

"Their cocks or their brains?"

Perhaps she'd been fond of neither.

"The companionship," I said.

"Ah, that. There's plenty of that to go around down here." She glugged, leaned forward, and said, "But there's always room for more."

Another Wife approached, dragging a tankard across the bar. It sang as it dipped and rose over the beaten surface. She wore a cocktail dress cinched around the waist with a length of rope.

"Hello ladies. Joining us, are you?"

I laughed at her, at the very idea of joining this crew. After all, my life was awaiting me. Wasn't it?

She reached over and placed her hand over Edna's. "I've been here ninety years, honey. Drunk the whole time. A swell drunk." She had the same expression as Shane—far off and easy. Though, too, she was clearly stimulated by the new company. I found I'd suddenly become jealous. For a start, I too wanted to place a hand over Edna's, and look upon her as if she were the most beautiful thing I'd seen in all these decades.

Wives continued to arrive and eventually formed a semicircle pressing in on us. I saw Edna assessing our new friends, scanning them from head to foot, getting their scent. As always, she was the overstimulated anthropologist. We were being welcomed, inoculated against time, purged of our earthly trajectory. I was intoxicated by then. And still am.

At some point we all rose and the women gave us a tour of their empire. Deep into the labyrinth of production facilities, we passed Alice. She was surrounded by a trio of burley Wives. Her beautiful hair had come half loose and was spilling down like a fountain. I was worried that it could be set ablaze in this place. A trade, I found out just minutes later that they were proposing a trade. Edna and I would stay and Alice would be released to live her life up top, sworn to secrecy. She didn't have the disposition to remain here, we later learned. She was too antsy and rebellious. We were meant to see her menaced, and came to understand that we are each the collateral for the other. None of it was necessary. In all likelihood I'd have stayed of my own free will, and Edna later said she'd have just blown shit up up top.

That night we were shown to our rooms, our creaky beds and squat dressers, all with the knots long popped out of the wood. Everything not of flesh ages so ungracefully down here.

Edna's eyes have lost their otherworldly sparkle, as if this were the other world for which they'd been designed. Even after all these years, we spend most nights together, wondering when we'll finally grow tired of each other.

Do I miss Ray? He was a caring and careful man, and had just perfected his recipe for sole *à la marinière*. I care about Ray, and I love sole *a là marinière*, but I know what my existence would have been up top: happy and finite. Soon the arc of my abandoned life will be a tiny temporal artifact, one divided by infinity. Our daughter, however, is another matter. She is like a phantom limb. Every night just before I drift off into the ether, I feel her suckling, letting me know of her presence and her absence. Frankly, I'm surprised by her persistence after so many years. Sometimes I want to be left alone and gently shoo her away; and sometimes I sing her a lullaby, hoping to keep the poor little thing, so warm and blubbery, close to my breast.

Years ago, during one of my after-shift wanderings, I discovered a small room with a grate set into its low ceiling, one of the places from which our facility draws its air. That room is the only place to go to feel the rain and sun and, so rarely, snow. When I go there, I duck beneath the grate, pitch my head back, and look toward the sky. Often I find that my sister is staring back down at me from her apartment three stories up. Her hair is beginning to go white, and the sun lights it up as she looks back down on me with a faint smile, making sure I'm okay.

Praise for *Motel Girl*

"Greg Sanders has hit the bullseye with *Motel Girl*. The stories—original, often surreal, yet thoroughly convincing—are tone-perfect, exuding a marvelous, full-bodied authority. An astonishingly fine debut."
—Janet Fitch

"Realistic absurdity ties together the short stories of Sanders's intelligent and funny collection."
—*Publishers Weekly*

"There is a kind of violence in every story, different kinds; and it is always surprising how the physical violence is the least disturbing kind."
—*Los Angeles Times*

"These stories are deft, enigmatic lyrics that pivot on an image or insight."
—*Rain Taxi Review of Books*

CPSIA information can be obtained
at www.ICGtesting.com
Printed in the USA
JSHW051017140222
22881JS00003B/183